BETTING
Blind

LILY GARDNER

DIVERSIONBOOKS

Diversion Books
A Division of Diversion Publishing Corp.
443 Park Avenue South, Suite 1008
New York, New York 10016
www.DiversionBooks.com

For more information, email info@diversionbooks.com

First Diversion Books edition March 2016.
Print ISBN: 978-1-68230-244-6
eBook ISBN: 978-1-62681-955-9

To both my Mikes and my dear friends and family who have sustained me through the writing of this book.

CHAPTER 1

Lennox Cooper went to retrieve her newspaper and found blood splattered over her front porch. It smelled like pancake syrup, and had a pink sheen that real blood didn't have. It had splashed across the floor and was dripping off her siding under the dining room windows. She picked up her bloody newspaper bag with thumb and forefinger and carried it, dripping, down the porch steps to the trash can by the garage. She left a trail of red blots. Lennox remembered the last shoot-out of her police career. The blood pooling beneath what was left of her partner's head onto the packed dirt yard behind the shooter's house. This memory was precisely what her dead partner's kid had intended. Cory Doran. Someone must have told Cory that Lennox bore part of the responsibility for his dad's death, and he was going to make damned sure she'd never forget it. As if she could.

Three spent balloons lay by the welcome mat. A crow stood in the street in front of Lennox's house picking at the fourth balloon. Lennox felt her gut sink like she'd swallowed a box of rocks, same as she felt every time Cory keyed her truck, or slashed her tires. She tried hard to pull in enough breath. The kid was never going to forgive Lennox. And why the hell should he?

It was already a problem having her office in her bungalow, so if the kid was going after her house, she'd have to figure out how to scrounge enough money to rent an office. In the meantime, she went downstairs for her scrub bucket and any cleanser that might work on red dye. She started on the siding. The red smeared and made a larger stain as she tried to wipe it up, the suds in her bucket now pink. It took her forever to mop it up, the syrupy smell turning her stomach. The longer she mopped, the guiltier she felt, until she wanted to dump the scrub water into the rhododendrons, and go back to bed.

It was after nine, and raining hard, before Lennox gave it up and went inside to get ready for a ten o'clock appointment, who showed up fifteen minutes early. Susan DeMarco was four inches taller than Lennox's five foot three. Her vintage clothes smelled of cigarette smoke, with a top note of eau-de-tavern. She was young and worried-looking. But who hires a detective if they're carefree? She seemed unduly impressed by Lennox's rubber plant and office furniture. How much did Lennox charge an hour?

Oh.

"Plus a retainer," Lennox said.

"How much?" De Marco said.

Lennox folded her hands on the desk, thinking this woman was never going to come up with the money to hire her. "First, let's hear your problem," she said.

De Marco twisted sideways in her chair. She had come to Lennox because a predator was going after her twelve-year-old son. Three weeks ago, she discovered a chain of emails between Richard and someone who was obviously a male adult, so she asked Richard about it. "He wasn't copping to any of it." De Marco canted her body in the other direction, her hands twitching in her lap. "I told him he had to drop this guy. I tried to explain to him that grown men make friends with other grown men, not with young boys.

"He didn't believe me, so I said I'd take away the laptop, his phone, everything if he didn't drop this guy immediately. He said he would. The thing is, I work nights at The Rialto. I don't even get home until three thirty in the morning. And he's still a child, even though he doesn't think so. Two days ago I found this same 'friend' on Richard's Facebook. He calls himself Rex Walker, but I don't know if that's his real name."

Lennox had never worked sex crimes when she was still a cop, but she knew these kind of cases pretty much ran the same way each time. Take a lonely kid, praise him, buy him shit, and pretty soon you had him in your pocket. Some kids didn't survive the abuse to make it to adulthood. They suicided or died by degrees using drugs or booze. The few survivors often became the next crop of abusers.

But the good news was that a predator often took months grooming a kid, gaining the child's trust before he tried anything. With luck, Lennox could get to this guy before he did any lasting damage.

"I'll need a $500 retainer," Lennox said. Like she could afford it, reducing her retainer to a quarter of what she normally charged. Lennox Cooper, the champion of single moms. There went the security deposit on a rented office. Jeez. "When can I talk to the boy?"

"Don't talk to him. No." De Marco pulled on her skirt, practically spazzing out. "He's not stupid. Couldn't you just go on his computer? Like, without him knowing?"

"Absolutely," Lennox told her, nodding like she was chock full of hacker expertise. She opened the center drawer of her desk and pulled out a key logger, and explained to Ms. De Marco how to plug it into the port, then plug his keyboard cable into the logger. "I'll pick it up on Wednesday," Lennox told her.

The key logger registered every keystroke the kid typed, from the time he came home from school on Monday afternoon until he left for school on Wednesday. There was plenty of correspondence between Richard and Rex Walker. Rex's real name was Ernie Foster, a divorced fifty-one-year-old insurance adjuster. His emails were full of gamer slang. They talked mostly about computer games and comic books. There was nothing sexual in any of their conversations, but Foster's approach was classic groomer. Here was a fifty-year-old guy using an alias, befriending a kid without clearing it with the kid's mother. The latest stats guessed that sixty percent of these guys were never popped, on account of the fact that their victims never told their parents. Most kids figured it was their fault. Foster had no criminal record. Yet.

Lennox started following Richard after school. Try tailing a kid who's on foot when you're in a car and then not getting pulled over for being a stalker yourself. But tailing someone was a task Lennox could do cross-eyed. She parked on Thirteenth Avenue off of Vermont. The minute she sighted Richard trudging home, she circled around to Florida Street. Then on to Chestnut. It took a week before she hit the jackpot: Richard being picked up by a late model BMW on Florida Street, Oregon license TVX197. Ernie Foster.

She followed them out of the burbs, across the bridge into northeast Portland. They pulled into a parking spot in front of a Vietnamese bridal shop. Lennox was able to park three cars behind them. Ernie had dressed in jeans and a black hoodie. A backward-facing baseball cap with a red-faced Hellboy embroidered on the crown hid his receding hairline. They walked three blocks past a microbrewery, a bike shop, a coffee shop. Cars splashed by on Sandy Boulevard. Rain shivered off the cherry trees planted by the curb. Ernie and Richard stopped in front of The Cosmic Monkey Comics, and entered.

An old fashioned bell rang as she followed them into the shop. This was nothing like the wire carousel at the front of the drugstore with the newest *Spider-man,* like when she was a kid. Portland took its comic books seriously. This was a good-sized bookstore with hardbound collections of comics, rare comics stored in plastic sleeves, graphic novels as vivid as tattoos. It smelled like the library from her childhood. She picked up a graphic novel, and paged through it while she checked out Richard and Ernie. They moved through the racks, Richard pulling out a book and looking to Ernie like, is this okay? And this? Ernie was smiling and nodding.

Then they were at the counter, Richard with a wide grin on his face and a stack of comics, Ernie with his arm around Richard's shoulder. It was all Lennox could do not to yell, *Get your hands off him!*

Richard asked the cashier when the next issue of *Deathstroke* was due.

"Not until May," the cashier said. A frail man, probably

the owner. He seemed to have trouble with his legs. But he smiled sympathetically at Richard. Two months is forever when you're a kid.

Ernie squeezed Richard's shoulder, then pulled out his wallet and paid for $48 worth of comics like he was buying a cappuccino. That was what these guys were like—little kids with grown-up resources, and happy to oblige.

"Hey Richard," Lennox said. "I'm a work friend of your mother's." She turned to Ernie and extended her hand. "Lennox Cooper."

She kept her eyes trained on Ernie. "Actually, Richard's mother hired me. I'm a detective. You're either Rex Walker or Ernie Foster, depending. Am I right?" She kept her attention focused on him. And half-expected him to collapse, start blubbering some version of *We're just friends*. When he didn't, she figured he'd bolt. She was positioned between the counter and the door, so he had to go through her to get out. Adrenaline was pinging along her nerve endings in the key of C.

He feinted right to get past her; she countered. He would have to go through her to escape. She was a whole lot smaller than him, but she looked like a cop. She watched him weigh his choices in less time than it took to draw a breath, then he lurched against the counter and punched the cashier in the face.

Where the fuck did that move come from? Lennox rushed around the counter, praying to God in heaven the man wasn't dead. More blood than was healthy was leaking out of him, but he was breathing. Pulse steady. Richard had backed against the book rack, crying. Lennox wadded up her jacket to elevate the old guy's head.

"Where's your cell?" she yelled at Richard. He patted

his pocket. He looked like he was in shock. She told him to call 911. "Now!" she said. "Tell them ambulance and police, tell them assault. Then stay put!"

Lennox was out the door.

Ernie had run a block by the time she made it to the street. She watched him turn right across the parking lot by Du's Grill. He plowed into people and knocked over umbrellas; his arms windmilled, and his gait uneven. This was a guy unaccustomed to running, but he had panic going for him. Lennox was the one with discipline. Her legs were way shorter than Ernie's, but she trained. Her pace was piston-like. Short be damned; she'd gain on his predatory ass. She just hoped he hadn't done permanent harm to the old shopkeeper.

She overtook Foster on Forty-sixth Avenue. She didn't give him a chance to surrender, just zapped him with the Taser. He crumpled, wordless, to the wet sidewalk. While he was incapacitated, she pulled his arms behind his back and cuffed him. Then she called the cops.

"AS3 Assault," she said. "Probable 163.434."

A few moments later Ernie caught his breath in a sob. And started weeping, his knees curled up to his chest. His hat lay on the sidewalk getting wet.

"We're just friends," he said, just like she'd figured he'd say. "Richard's like my son, Eric."

"Bullshit," she said. "If you were innocent, why the alias? Why didn't you ask permission from his mother? Why did you near kill the old man?"

Ernie broke into a fit of weeping, tears and snot streaming down his face. "I lost my boy."

"Shut up," she said. "I'm holding you until the police get here. You can tell them your sad fucking story."

She sounded tough. Her gut said he was a predator, and she had to go with that. There wasn't a cop alive that didn't trust her gut. They're dealing with humanity 24-7: people trying to get away with shit, crazy people, drunk people, and people high on drugs. If a cop gets an impression or has a funny feeling, she'd be a fool not to go with it. So maybe she wasn't a cop anymore. But those eight years with the Portland Police were in her psyche, her reflexes—she'd never get it out.

A squad car pulled to the curb and hauled Ernie Foster away. Lennox kept hearing him protest that he and Richard were just friends. Of course he'd say that, the freak. Lennox hoped the cops threw the book at him. He'd assaulted that old man, and was grooming a little kid to be his lover. Lennox did the right thing.

Yeah, she did the right thing.

CHAPTER 2

Friday night poker at the Shanty Bar and Grill.

Poker night was the sweetest spot in Lennox's week. Dim light, air heavy with the smell of fried clams and spilled microbrew. The Shanty was older than most of the neighborhood. Opinions varied as to when the cops from Northeast Precinct adopted the bar. The owner claimed off-duty policemen were throwing down shots and beers back when he bought the place in the '70s.

The cops sitting shoulder to shoulder at the Shanty started in with the razz the minute Lennox walked in the door.

One cop shouted, "Meanie!" The guys sitting closest to him broke into a chorus of "Waahhhh." They'd heard about her collar, heard that the predator had bust out sobbing like a child.

Someone yelled, "Way to go, Dickless Tracy. Making a grown man cry."

Every cop in the bar laughed at her. Lennox had known a lot of these guys more than a decade, from back when she was a cop. There'd been a time when most of them hated her. They blamed her for her partner's death. Nowadays a few of them liked her well enough to give her shit.

Lennox painted a faint grin on her face and, eyes forward, marched to the back room. She opened the door to the game.

The five guys she played poker with were her tribe. They'd stuck by her when she screwed up, watched over her, flattered her, and over the years lost a boatload of money to her. They were all connected to law enforcement, one way or another.

Ham jumped to his feet, toppling over his stack of red chips. They clicked against each other so delectably, she wanted to snatch one and put it between her teeth. Ham had just gotten a haircut, and his Berkeley warm-up jacket looked freshly laundered. It took months of complaint before he'd get that jacket cleaned. He said the dry cleaning chemicals interfered with his luck. Ham had taught her how to play poker her sophomore year at Berkeley. She'd learned a lot more about human nature and the laws of probability at the poker table than in a classroom. She didn't like school all that much, but she finished her undergraduate degree in psychology, then went back to Portland to the police academy. Ham stayed on at Berkeley for graduate school. As soon as he moved to Portland, they resumed their Friday night poker game. She had been Ham's best man at his wedding.

"Lennox, do you remember Frank? He went to college with us?"

She did not, which was odd because he was pretty darned cute—dark-haired and scrubbed, with a square chin and a muscular neck. Frank was on his feet as well. "Frank

Cardo," he said. He held her hand a little too long, and his face kind of went soft and melty. Had he been this adorable at school?

"Don't let her ponytail fool you," Fish said. "She's the toughest player at the table."

"Oh," Frank said. And made an attempt to pull himself together.

An old guy sitting next to Fish under the neon beer sign had to be a relative: low forehead and hair thick enough to break a comb. Only the old guy had gone gray.

"Greg, aren't you going to introduce me?" said the old guy. Greg was Fish, so called because he'd attached a magnetic Jesus fish to his squad car back in his patrol days. Fish introduced his uncle from San Francisco.

Two new players. New players meant new money. Fresh meat.

Lennox said howdy to Fish's uncle and took the empty chair next to Frank. Settled so that her thigh almost grazed his when she crossed her legs. Felt his attention like pinpricks. Smelled his department store aftershave. For the record, he smelled pretty great.

What was it going to be: lucky in love, or lucky in cards? If she played it right, the two newcomers could hand over enough poker winnings to make up for the deep discount she'd given her newest client. On the other hand, a new boyfriend might be just the thing. The last affair she'd had was a year ago. Not only were she and the ex no longer on speaking terms, their families weren't on speaking terms. From old family friends to the Capulets and the Montagues. It was enough to make any woman think twice before dating again.

"Did you see Fulin out in the bar?" Jerry asked her.

She had not. Fulin Chen worked as a parole officer. Fulin was six feet tall with black hair that swung in a braid past his tight little tush. Why she'd turned him down the couple of times he made a play for her was one of life's mysteries, like who built the pyramids.

"Where the hell is he?" Jerry reached in his tweed jacket for his cell. "I'll try him again." Old Jerry's face was as creased as his shirt, and his ginger hair was mostly gray. Jerry dated women half his age, but he had more kindness and old-fashioned chivalry than a dozen men. A minute later he slipped the phone back in his pocket. "He's not picking up."

"He never misses a game," Sarge said. Lennox would swear that he polished that bald head of his. He wore a mustache, the ends waxed into neat little points. Everything about Sarge was trim and tidy. He ran the evidence room for the cop shop and was Lennox's inside man on a lot of deals. Sarge was old enough to retire, but then what would he do? Edge his lawn twice a week?

Ham, Fish, Jerry, Fulin, Sarge: her guys.

The new men didn't know who this Fulin character was. Didn't care. They turned to the dealer. That would be Ham. Nothing got between Ham and his poker game, not even Fulin missing in action. Ham sucked the beer off his mustache with his teeth, and ran his thumbnail under the seal on a deck of cards.

Nothing like a fresh deck of cards, the rasp they make as they slide against each other. The clatter like bones as the dealer shuffles. If you get cards you know that feeling. Then the dealer hands you a brand new pattern, and you're in the game.

Today it was Texas Hold'em. Ham dealt each player two

cards down. Lennox peeked. She was looking at garbage. She recrossed her legs.

The blinds threw in their chips. She folded along with Ham and Fish. Jerry checked. Sarge threw in a chip; the grumpy uncle threw in two.

Frank raised. Grumpy reraised. The rest of the table called. Ham dealt the turn card. Katy, the cocktailer, cracked the door of the poker room. Lennox ordered a Jack Daniels sour.

Check. Raise. Chips tossed in the middle of the table. Lennox reached for her bag on the floor between her and Frank and located her lipstick. Frank got twitchy. She took her sweet time getting her lips just right. She could rob this guy blind.

She peeked over her mirror, saw Fish giving her the stink eye. "Why don't you make yourself useful, Cooper, get us fries or something."

"See if Fulin's picking up," Ham said.

"He's fine. He's an adult," she said, but thought, what if he was in an accident? Sarge was right; Fulin never missed a game.

The uncle slapped his cards down. "I thought we were going to play real cards here," he said to Fish.

Showdown. Frank laid out his three of a kind. Okay, so he had the cards, but his betting was artless. If she'd had his cards, she would've called the first round, maybe raised the second, aggressed more with each round.

Sarge dealt. Once again, her hole cards were excrement. Patience was a muscle Lennox had developed over the years, whether it was as she waited for her cards to warm up or sat in her Bronco for three long days running surveillance. Grumpy smiled and threw in three chips.

"In the city we play no-limit," he said. The city being big-time San Francisco.

Fish made eye contact. If she was any good at reading body language—and she was—she'd say Fish was giving her permission to have her way with his uncle. If she could just get some cards.

The betting went around the table. Jerry folded after the turn. Going to the john, he said. Going to call Fulin, she figured. She was beginning to worry about Fulin, too. Nine years she'd been playing with Fulin, and he'd never missed a game.

By the third hand, she had a low pair in the hole. Just enough to play, but her luck was thin and limp. Her friends called or raised; she had their game memorized and she'd pretty much sussed out the newcomers as well. Grumpy played a tight game, going for the high hands. He played the odds, bet what he had, and no more. It was a joyless way to play, and made it hard to take much off him, but he had a weakness: he'd raise if he thought one of the guys was bluffing him. Delicious, if she could just get some cards she could work with, and get them to bet the moon. Then she'd show them how it was done, Portland style.

Hand after hand for the next hour and a half, the ice in her drink melting, her cards going from ice-cold to tepid. It was like the new guys had sucked up all the luck in the room and sat wasting it on their bullshit bets. Still, Frank was up a hundred bucks. She'd left off trying to flirt with him.

They took a break to stretch, use the facilities, and get more drinks. Jerry punched a number on his cell, listened, then pocketed his phone. "I don't get it."

"His parents are super old," she said. "Maybe one of them went to the hospital."

Frank walked up behind her. Put a warm hand on her shoulder and bent down to her ear. "What are you doing after the game?" he whispered.

"Depends," she said. She had to admit, she'd liked him better before she started playing cards with him. And it wasn't really his fault. She just hated playing with people luckier than her.

Ham joined them with a pint of the Shanty's signature beer, the Hop-ness Monster. "Ready for some cards?"

They sat down. Sarge dealt. And there it was. Between her hole cards and the flop she had two pair, kings and jacks. A surge of dopamine flooded her nervous system, tickling the hell out of her pleasure centers. She closed her hand and crossed her legs. Called when the betting came to her. Sarge dealt the turn card. She shifted weight from one buttock to the other. Looked tentative. She met the next raise and bumped it. Raised the limit on the river card, a king, but kept her face neutral with a touch of timidity. She looked up through her eyelashes at the old man. Grumpy didn't believe for one second that she had the chops. Sure enough, he redoubled. Now it was Frank's turn to look uncomfortable. He was ninety bucks into the hand. If he folded he'd look the fool, but it was clear as clear he didn't have the cards. He called.

She spread her full house, kings over jacks, and scooped the pot. She'd made up for the first half of the game and was solidly back in the black.

Fish dealt the next hand. Her cell phone vibrated against her hip. She looked at the screen. "It's Fulin."

"Answer it!" the guys said in chorus.

"Fulin, I'm in the middle of a game here. Where the hell are you?"

"Need a ride," Fulin said.

She asked him if he was drunk. He sounded drunk. His words slid over one another. He told her he needed $300 for bail.

Fulin told her they wouldn't let him take a cab. "They" were the good folks at the Multnomah County Jail.

"Holy shit," she said. "Do they know you're a cop?"

He mumbled something.

"What did you do?" she said.

Static over the phone. "I'm in trouble, Lennox," he said. "Please."

Fuck! And fuck again! She'd go. Of course she'd go. He needed help. She was there for him, no matter how he'd trashed her night. "I'm coming," she said.

"You," Fulin said. "Nobody else."

The guys stared at her, waiting for her to tell them.

She tossed her cards down and turned to Ham. "Cash me out," she said.

She told them Fulin had got himself in a scrape, but he was okay. Told them he didn't want any company. Just her.

"We're in a middle of a hand," Grumpy said.

She had her jacket on and was stuffing money into her wallet.

"Maybe later?" Frank said.

He wasn't just good-looking; he gave the impression he was sturdy and kind and clean-cut. Lennox wondered what it would be like to date a guy like that. She smiled and palmed him her business card.

CHAPTER 3

Lennox rolled around all the possibilities that would've landed Fulin Chen in jail, and came up with nothing. If he had a temper, she'd never seen it. He wasn't a heavy drinker; he wasn't the kind of guy who engaged in nefarious activities.

She drove down Sandy, dodging the blinking lights of cyclists who drifted into her lane. It had quit raining for the moment. The cloud cover shone pink from the city lights. It was ten at night when Lennox crossed the Burnside Bridge, the lights from the Morrison and Hawthorne Bridges reflected in the black water of the Willamette River. Once she crossed the bridge, she was downtown.

A Friday night in Portland in March when it was not pissing down rain was as rare as rare. Everyone in the city was out and about. People crowded the sidewalks, queuing in front of the food carts that bordered Second Avenue. Lennox had to dodge cyclists and jay-walkers before she found a place to park. The jail looked as busy as the nightclubs, a flow of family members climbing the steps past security into the gray granite lobby of the Multnomah County Jail.

Doris was manning the desk when Lennox stepped up to post bail.

"Isn't this your card night?" Doris asked. Her crew cut as gray as the decor.

Lennox nodded and shrugged. What are you going to do when the kid's in jail? She handed Doris the bail and tucked the receipt in her pocket. Lennox heard a pneumatic hiss, a door opened, and out shuffled Fulin Chen. One of his eyes was sealed shut, and his lip was swollen.

"Oh jeez, Fulin, what happened to you?" she said.

He shook his head, then realized shaking was not a good move. A bruise darkened his cheekbone.

She stood next to him while he completed the checkout, then walked out with him into the cold March night.

"Thanks," he mumbled. And grunted in pain as he climbed into the Bronco's cab.

"What happened to you?" she said.

"I'm in bad trouble," his voice slurred from his swollen lip.

"No doubt. What's your boss going to say when she finds out you've been arrested?"

She glanced over at him. He had his hands braced on his knees. His head was down. "They're calling it assault, but it's a whole lot worse."

Lennox knew by his tone: Chen was telling it true. It scared her, like what he was about to say would change everything. They'd crossed the Steel Bridge back to the east side. Without asking him, she parked the truck by the river. He moved stiffly as they walked the wide steps down to the Esplanade, a series of boardwalks and floating docks, benches, and sculpture that ribboned along the riverbank and under the freeway overpass. They stopped and sat on a bench facing the water. The benches were still damp from the afternoon rain. The moon appeared behind a ragged cloud and added its light to the city's neon reflecting off the river.

"Tell me," she said.

He had a client, Matilda Bauer. Late twenties, liked to sleep with married men, steal their credit cards, charge them to the moon, and sign using their wives' names. It worked like a charm until it didn't. Bauer did a three-year stay at the Copper River Women's Penitentiary, and eventually landed as one of Fulin's parolees.

"What's that got to do with you getting beat on and arrested?"

"She no-showed for our ten o'clock this morning," Fulin said. "I called her house, called her work. Nothing. After work I paid a visit to her house." But Matilda wasn't home. Her mom told him she was spending the weekend with a girlfriend. Before Fulin could get back in his car this punk came out of nowhere, swinging a baseball bat. Fulin tried to keep from getting nailed by the bat, using his kung fu moves on the guy. Then the cops came.

"Why would the punk come after you?" she said.

"I guess he was the boyfriend."

"What are you saying? You slept with her?" She stood up and walked further down the dock. This disgusting situation had cost her a night's poker winnings. She turned back to him. "You owe me $500: three for bail and two for what it cost me to leave the card table. I want it by the end of the weekend, and I'm not kidding, Chen."

"I didn't touch her!" Fulin's voice cracked. A couple walking past glanced first at Fulin, then at her.

"I would've never laid a hand on her."

"Then why?" Lennox said.

"Sit down," Fulin said. "I can't talk to you when you're pacing."

Lennox reluctantly seated herself next to him. Watched the reflection of the green lights from the Hawthorne Bridge reflected in the water. She had a lot of nerve getting on her high horse over Fulin bonking a client. She'd slept with a fellow police officer for three years, and he was married.

Fulin's battered face was deep in shadow. He touched his lip carefully. It had started bleeding again. Lennox handed him a tissue. "I signed up on one of those online dating sites," he said.

"Why?" she said. "You could have anyone you want."

He turned toward her, regarded her with his good eye. "You could have anyone you want."

"It's different," she said.

"No," he said. "It's exactly the same."

She so did not want to go down this road. "My love life is not the point," she said. "Tell me what online dating has got to do with your client."

"You remember me talking about Lynn?"

Of course. Endlessly. He bugged everyone to death with her image on his phone.

"It was all a fake," Fulin said. "She wore a wig and different makeup. I don't know, maybe she photoshopped herself. You'd never guess it was the same woman."

"You're saying Lynn is Matilda? Fulin, how could you not know that?"

"I never actually met her. In the flesh." He rubbed his temple, then groaned.

This was big trouble. At the very least, his supervisor would think he was a gormless dumbfuck. At most, he could end up like Lennox, excommunicated and forced to reinvent himself.

"Why would she do that?" Lennox said. "The last person you want to mess with is your parole officer."

"She wanted me to cover for her, say that she attended her appointments with me, that she worked steady and kept her nose clean. I never told her I would do it."

"You've got to go to your supervisor, Fulin," she said. "You've got to tell her what Matilda's trying to pull. And you've got to write her up."

A yacht passed through the colored reflections on the river. A few minutes later, its wake lapped up against the floating dock.

Fulin, the man with the martial arts posture, slumped over like his bones had melted.

"I have been covering for her for the last month," he said. "Tonight I went over to her house to tell her I was done with this. If it cost me my job, I was done."

"And you got yourself arrested. You can see what's happening here," she said. "The longer you wait, the messier this thing gets."

"You're right. I just need to find her," he said. "Can you help me? I'll hire you."

The way he was acting, Lennox got that itchy feeling. The Bauer woman had more on Fulin than a handful of mushy emails.

"You need a retainer?" he said. "I know it's the weekend, do you get more money on the weekend?" His voice pitched higher. "We've got to find her right away. Before Monday, can you do that?"

"Sure," she said. "Now tell me what she's got on you."

Fulin clasped his hands together and shoved them

between his legs, then noticed what he was doing and folded his arms across his chest. "We had cyber sex. She screen captured it. Or something, I don't know. She has pictures."

Man, this was bad. Very bad.

She'd find the Bauer chick one way or another. Still, once Lennox found her, it was Matilda's word against Fulin's as to whether they had sex. And unless Fulin had a horseshoe up his ass, his career in law enforcement would be over before the end of the year.

"Can you drive me to Matilda's?" he said.

"Jesus, Fulin. Are you kidding me?"

"No way in hell I'm leaving my Beamer in that neighborhood," he said.

Fulin's car was parked in front of a little house north of Killingsworth. The car looked a whole lot better than Fulin. He heaved a sigh of relief. She told him to take it easy getting home. She'd call as soon as she had any news.

On the drive home, her cell phone rang. It was Frank Cardo. Frank said the game went late, but they could still meet somewhere, he knew a nice little club with good jazz.

"Not tonight," she said. "This thing with my friend, it got complicated." It was complicated, and she was exhausted.

"Sure," he said. "I get it. What about dinner tomorrow?"

Maybe the bad luck she'd had at the table tonight was love knocking on the door. What else could she do but humbly accept the laws of chance? She told him yes, she'd like that very much.

CHAPTER 4

Rain fell in sheets from the low-bellied clouds. It was eleven o'clock on a Saturday morning. Lennox pulled up to the Bauer residence and ran to the house. It was a one-and-a-half story English cottage, half-hidden by two enormous rhododendron bushes. Lennox stood under the tiny roof of the stoop, getting damper and colder by the second. Matilda's mother answered the door on the fourth ring. She was a short, plump hen of a woman, dressed in lavender sweat pants and a matching hoodie.

"Are you Rose Bauer?" Lennox asked.

Lennox introduced herself, showed the old lady her investigative license. "Matilda missed her appointment with her parole officer Friday morning. I'm assisting him in trying to locate her. Is she home?"

Rose's kind face shifted to guarded. "I told Fulin that Mattie went to her girlfriend's house," Rose said. "That's all I know."

"Do you know her girlfriend's name?"

"Her name is Debbie. I don't know her last name, or

her phone number. Mattie's not a child; she goes where she pleases."

Lennox shivered under the eave of the Bauer house. She was getting soaked.

"May I come in?" she said. "I just have a few more questions."

It took a few moments for Rose to decide before unlocking the storm door and letting Lennox into the living room. The furniture was upholstered entirely in blue, the sofa flanked by lamps that sprung from faux butter churns. Two brass eagles graced the fireplace mantle next to framed photos of a high-school-aged Matilda. Everything was clean as clean. An ironing board was positioned in front of the television.

Rose told Lennox to sit down, then chose an overstuffed velour chair opposite her.

"Last night after Fulin Chen spoke to you," Lennox said, "he was attacked by a man. Late twenties, blonde?"

"Joey Tufts." The old lady spat the name.

"A friend of Matilda's?" Lennox said.

"Something like that."

"This is a difficult question to ask," Lennox said. She hesitated a second. "I wondered if you were the person who called the police on Joey and Fulin."

The old lady reddened. "I had to. I like Fulin, but they were killing each other in my front yard."

"Do you have any idea why Joey went after Fulin?"

"Jealousy, I suppose. Joey's been crazy for Mattie since he was a little kid."

"Do you know why Joey would think Fulin was a competitor?"

Rose got this world-weary expression that didn't go

with her sweet old lady face.

"I've seen a lot of people go stupid over Mattie."

"You're wrong about Fulin," Lennox said. "He just wants to keep Mattie from going back to prison. She broke her parole when she didn't keep her appointment yesterday. I want to find her, impress on her how important it is she show up for her Monday appointment."

"Impress on her?" Rose snorted. "You don't know Mattie. She'll do what she's going to do."

"Look, Rose, let me try to find her. Maybe she has an address book in her room?"

Rose shook her head. "Mattie would have a fit if she knew anyone had been in her bedroom."

"I'm a detective," Lennox said. "I won't disturb a thing."

"You don't think Mattie knows that skipping her appointment will break the conditions of her parole?"

"Fulin's already stuck his neck out," Lennox said.

Rose shrugged. Lennox had seen this attitude before. Dollars to donuts, Rose had spent major time at Al-Anon meetings, learning how not to let her children destroy her.

She opened a door off the living room and pointed to a narrow flight of stairs, then turned the television up.

The top of the stairs opened into Matilda's room. It had originally been an attic space with a gabled end facing the street. The windows were framed in white ruffled curtains, the knee walls papered in faded blue flowers. A pale blue chest decoupaged with Little Mermaid figures stood in the corner of the painted floor; old dolls sat crammed together on a bookshelf over a child's stool. A large standing mirror faced a narrow bed. An office desk and two metal four-drawer file cabinets stood against the far wall.

File cabinets in a bedroom? Matilda worked as an

admin at a high-tech business. No business would let her keep files at home.

Lennox tried a drawer. Locked. All the drawers were locked.

Lennox rummaged through her bag, pulled out a pick, and unlocked the top drawer.

Three wigs—a very long black wig with bangs, and two brown wigs, one short and curly, one shoulder-length and wavy. The next drawer was filled with blonde wigs. Auburn, pink, silver. The other file cabinet was stuffed with costumes: garter belts, leather collars, studded bras, and leopard print leggings. Underneath a pair of crotchless panties, Lennox found a red leather flogger. It was so odd: the dolls, the Little Mermaid, and all the costumes.

Likely the answer to all Matilda's secrets was filed on her computer. Lennox walked over to Matilda's display, which stretched the width of her desk. Matilda's laptop lay closed in front of it. Lennox pulled out the external drive from her bag and plugged it into the laptop.

Matilda's computer asked for a password.

Lennox typed *123456*.

Password?

She tried all the standard passwords: *qwerty, master, blahblah, testing, biteme,* and *whatever. Matrix, secret, help me, princess.*

Not princess. Lennox glanced at Bauer's toy chest. She typed *LittleMermaid.*

Score.

Feeling pretty damn smug, Lennox started a copy of the whole hard drive. While her external drive captured the files, Lennox used her pick to break into Matilda's desk. Photos. Posed pictures, candids, the faces smiling, looking hopeful. People who were not related to each other by the look of them, but she needed to know for sure.

While her drive kept copying files, Lennox scooped up a stack of the photographs and descended the narrow steps.

A stack of dishtowels squatted on the butt end of Rose's ironing board. On the television, a young couple toasted one another with champagne flutes.

Rose looked up from the dishtowels, steam hissing from her iron. The smell of hot cotton filled the room. Matilda kept dog collars and floggers in her childhood bedroom, and her mother ironed her dishtowels.

"Are you finished?" Rose said.

"Almost," Lennox said. "If I could I show you these photos?" She held the first one in front of Rose. "Are they relatives or maybe Matilda's friends?"

Rose took the stack and thumbed through several photos, then spread the rest across the length of her ironing board. "I've never seen these people before." She piled the photos back in a stack. "You said you were looking for an address book. I didn't give you permission to go through all her things."

"I'm ready to leave," Lennox said. "I'll just get my bag upstairs and be on my way."

"I hope you've left her room the way you found it," Rose said.

Lennox reassured her. Said she'd be down in a minute. She climbed the steps back up to Matilda's childhood room. Returned the photos to the drawer and stirred them so they looked the same way she'd found them. Who were these people?

Matilda went to prison for seducing married men and stealing from them. Now she kept a locked file cabinet full of wigs and costumes. Matilda tricked Fulin and left him facing termination, possibly rape if she accused him of having sex with her. This was not a reformed woman.

Lennox looked at Matilda's computer screen. The download was complete. How many of those photos in her desk drawer were her victims?

Leave the room the way you found it.

Lennox disconnected her external drive, then pulled a thumb drive from her bag, plugged it in, copied over the program, and typed "run wipeout."

Said adios to Matilda's hard drive.

CHAPTER 5

It was still raining by the time Lennox got back to her office from the Bauer house. She watched a nuthatch pick through the sunflower husks beneath her empty bird feeder. She waited for her external drive to download Matilda's data. What kind of a character was this Matilda? She'd blown off her job and her parole officer to hang out with a girlfriend for the weekend. Why not wait until after work? Was she testing the limits of what she could get away with, or was there something more important going on with this friend of hers?

The first thing to do was go through the address book. Three Debbies came up, but only one was local: Debbie Paulson.

Paulson answered on the third ring. She sounded like an older woman.

"I'm looking for Matilda Bauer," Lennox said.

Debbie hung up. Not only older, but totally rude. It wasn't like Lennox was trying to sell the woman a credit card or urge her to vote Republican.

Lennox dialed her number again.

"This is very important," Lennox said, rushing her words before she was hung up on again. "Matilda's mother said she was at your house."

"She's not here anymore," Debbie said. There was a tiny pause in the line, only a millisecond.

"Wait," Lennox said. "Matilda's in trouble. Do you have any idea where she could be?"

"What kind of trouble?"

"If I don't find her by Monday, a bench warrant goes out for her arrest."

"No," Debbie said. "That's got nothing to do with me." The phone went dead again.

So much for that lead. Matilda had been at Debbie's and left some time before Saturday afternoon—not on good terms, from the sound of things. Who else would know her whereabouts? Rose didn't know of any friends other than Debbie. That left Joey Tufts, the boyfriend. Lennox made a call and learned that he was still a guest at the county jail.

Ten minutes on the computer gave her a little background on Joey. The guy had the world's cutest mug shot. He looked like a Renaissance angel, with gold curls and round blue eyes. He'd enjoyed two stays for felony theft at the Sheridan Correctional Facility. He also had been charged with assault three times, and all three times the charges were dropped. Lennox looked at her watch. Plenty of time to have a chat with Joey, hopefully get some idea of Matilda's whereabouts, and get home in time to clean up for her hot date.

Lennox called Fulin and asked him if he wanted to put up money for Tufts' bail. It involved some argument, but eventually Fulin agreed.

Twenty minutes later Lennox was handing Doris, the desk cop, the bail money.

"Twice in twenty-four hours," Doris said. "You a bond bailsman now?"

She shook her head. "Still a PI."

"Well watch out for this character," Doris said. "He's not a nice boy like Fulin."

Lennox leaned against the granite wall while Joey's paperwork was processed. Joey was tall and lanky like Fulin, but with blond hair that curled over his collar and into his eyes. His nose was broken, and both eyes were nearly swollen shut. Joey had been the guy with the baseball bat, and he looked worse than Fulin.

Doris pointed to Lennox, and Joey looked over at her. He gave her as game a smile as he could given the condition of his face. He walked stiffly over to her.

"Who are you?" he said.

"I'm Lennox, Mattie's friend. She asked me to bail you out."

"You going to give me a ride home?" he said. He had a very low voice.

Lennox's nervous system amped up to alert status. She pulled her jacket collar up closer to her neck. It wasn't only that he was dangerous. She could tell she hadn't sold him on being Matilda's friend.

"Let's get the hell out of here," she said.

Diagonals of cold rain fell across Third Avenue. It was nearly five, but with the rain they had skipped the sunset and gone straight to nighttime. They hiked the two blocks to her truck in the dark, passing a handful of pedestrians under black umbrellas. She unlocked the Bronco, stuffed her bag under her seat, and wiped the fogged windshield with her sleeve. Cold air blasted through the vents.

"Where do you live?" she asked Joey.

"Didn't Mattie tell you?"

"No," she said. "And now she's not answering her phone. I called her house. Her mother said she was at Debbie's, but I called there and she'd left. Do you know where else she could be?"

"Never heard of Debbie," he said.

"What about her other friends?" she said.

"Never heard of you."

"I'm a friend from work," she said. "Mattie's very popular at work."

He patted his pockets. "Do you have a cigarette?"

"No." She turned into traffic. "Where to?"

"East side," he said. "115th off Foster."

Felony Flats.

Felony Flats was not called that to be funny. More ex-felons lived in the long stretch of scrubland in East County than anywhere in the city. As for theft, you were taking your chances leaving a locked car on the street. And the best thing you could say about the housing out there was it was affordable.

She headed south to the Ross Island Bridge and across to the east side.

"Where do you think Mattie could've gone?" she said.

"Don't know." He didn't sound very curious either. "Pretty nice of you to go to the jail on a Saturday. Bail me out and all."

He was on to her. He'd been on to her from the beginning. "I'm glad to do it," she said. "Only I need that bail money back before Monday because of bills I got to pay. Mattie said she'd have the money for me tonight."

"Uh-huh," he said. He didn't sound surprised that Matilda would promise to pay back a debt and disappear.

Lennox headed east on Powell Boulevard. It started raining harder. Chain grocery stores and the strip malls they anchored were replaced by putty colored apartment buildings. Then vacant lots, pick-and-pull junkyards, strip joints. She had left southeast Portland and was headed into East County.

They approached the Copper Penny, a bar known for its generous drinks and rowdy clientele. Two dog walkers were silhouetted in the neon from the bar's sign.

Lennox glanced at her watch.

"You in a hurry?" Joey said.

"I've got a date—" she started to say. She was driving one second and the next second Joey had grabbed the steering wheel and pulled the Bronco over the curb and onto the sidewalk. Both dog walkers ran for their lives, hauling their dogs along with them, the walkers screaming, the dogs barking their heads off.

"What the fuck?" Lennox shouted. Her heart bumped against her ribs, her fingers still clutching the steering wheel. Joey unsnapped his seatbelt and twisted his body so he was half on top of her. Snatched her bag from under the truck seat and sat back down.

She lunged for the bag, but he blocked her with his elbow.

"What the hell are you doing?" she said.

He dumped the bag.

Her tools spilled over his lap and onto the truck floor. Her camera, her telephoto lens, her buck knife, picks, wallet, handcuffs.

"This is some pretty weird shit for a secretary," he said.

He flipped open her wallet. "You're working for that ninja bastard that busted my nose."

He shoved his door open, jumped out of the truck, scattering her ID and tools all over the street and sidewalk. The last she saw of him, he was running into the night.

• • •

Frank climbed down her porch steps, looking damp, cold, and pissed off. She ran up to him with her wet hair, house keys in hand, a string of apologies falling out of her mouth.

"I tried calling you," Frank said.

"I was giving this guy a ride," she said. "Then he dumped my bag out on the truck floor. My phone fell on the sidewalk and cracked. I'm not sure if it's broken or the battery is just loose."

He got this look on his face like he was willing to give her the benefit of the doubt. "Let me look at it," he said. He followed her into the house.

She emptied her bag on the dining room table. Her phone lay in two pieces.

He took off his jacket and draped it over a dining room chair. She towel dried her hair, then trotted in the kitchen for the wine. Nothing like a cabernet to smooth over the rough edges, a bad day, an almost-aborted date. She handed Frank a glass. He handed her her phone, its case a little scratched, but in one piece. She pressed the redial, and Frank's phone rang.

"Thanks," she said.

"You pick up hitchhikers?" Frank said.

She told him how she was trying to locate Matilda.

"You're lucky you didn't get hurt," he said. And he

looked scared. Like he'd accidentally found himself hanging out with the wrong crowd. Like maybe he considered *her* part of the wrong crowd.

"Ham told you I used to be a cop, right?"

His eyes widened, and he gave his head a little shake. "No," he said. "Wow. I've never dated a cop before."

She tried to get a read on him. If they were playing cards, she'd say he wasn't betting on a sure thing. And she was wondering if she had more balls than this guy. Now it was her turn to be pissed off. "We don't have go through with this," she said.

"With what?"

"Dinner," she said. "You seem to be having second thoughts."

"What? No!" he said. "It just seems so dangerous. And you don't look like the type."

Lennox could've asked him what type of woman he was envisioning. But to ask could very well derail the evening. And truth be told, she wanted dinner. And more wine. And male company. Sometimes it was better to have dinner with a nice man than to know the nice man's opinions on every little thing.

* * *

They'd polished off a bottle of wine and finished half the entree when Lennox's cell phone vibrated against her hip. She startled, but didn't pull the phone out of her pocket. Three minutes later, the phone went off again. The second time, Frank asked her if she was going to answer it. She told him sorry and looked at the screen. It was Fulin.

"Go ahead and answer it," he said.

Fulin was a mess. Saturday night and no clue where Matilda could've gotten herself to. Lennox kept catching Frank's eye, raising a finger, *just one minute*. "She could've left the state," Fulin said. Lennox told him it was unlikely. Matilda would've returned home and packed a bag. "Fulin," she said. "I'm having dinner. I'll call you when I get home."

"Sorry," she told Frank again. "These parole skips are the devil."

What she just said was bullshit. She'd never done a parole skip before. Truth was, whether she was working surveillance, missing persons, fraud, or homicide, the work took over her life.

Her salmon had turned cold. Her phone rang again.

"You better get that," Frank said. It was old lady Kurtz from across the street. A couple of juvenile delinquents were vandalizing Lennox's house.

Frank finished the last inch of wine at the bottom of his glass. Then smiled at her, a moist, disappointed little smile. "I guess we better get you home," he said.

And she agreed.

CHAPTER 6

Lennox had the old nightmare, the one that had kept coming back for the past two years. Only this time, a phone rang from the meth-head's house. It rang for hours, through the screaming and the gunshots. The phone was still ringing when Lennox woke up, the light from her bedroom windows dim, the corners of her room still in shadow. It was either very early in the morning or raining again. She picked up the phone.

"Bauer missed her seven thirty," Fulin said, his voice so whispery Lennox could barely make it out.

"Did you call her work?"

Of course he had. Out sick, they'd said. No answer at the house. Lennox had combed through Matilda's data, and called every number that was local trying to track down someone who knew Matilda's whereabouts. A friend, maybe, just a real person who she might have talked to. All she'd been able to ferret out from Matilda's data was a list of eight guys she was blackmailing and a patchwork of emails and chatrooms where she flirted under various aliases and images, not all of them female. And never Matilda's real image. Bottom line, the only people in town Lennox could go to apart from the people Matilda was blackmailing were Debbie Paulson, Joey, Rose, and the women Matilda worked with.

Fulin was booked with clients until five thirty that afternoon. "Matilda's left the state, I know it," he said.

It was sure looking that way.

There was a long pause. She heard him breathing into the phone. "What am I going to do?" he whispered.

Lennox pulled her robe on with her free hand and told Fulin he had to suck it up, tell his boss he'd been set up, tell her he hadn't done anything unethical.

"I told you," he hissed into the phone. "I've fudged her records for the last month. You've got to find her. My boss is zero tolerance. The old man told me not to buy the car. Now I'm screwed."

Lennox asked him about the union. But she knew the answer to that one. He'd get pink-slipped before you could say "sexual impropriety."

"Today," he said in a low voice. "Tomorrow I'll have to issue the warrant."

Fulin had said no later than Monday, and now he was saying Tuesday. The desperation tightened his vocal cords.

"I'll go to Matilda's workplace, see if someone down there has any ideas," she said. Then promised she'd call Fulin if she had any leads whatsoever.

• • •

When you're a cop, if you show a person your badge, you're as good as in. And if you make an appointment with the person, and they flake on you, you've got recourse. When you're a PI, it's best not to make appointments. Nine out of ten times they'll no-show, and there's not a damn thing you can to do about it.

Lennox decided to make a personal call.

Matilda worked at Geitner Graphics, a high-tech business located west of downtown in the area known as the Silicon Forest. A forest populated with miles and miles of two-story office buildings, and acres and acres of parking lots. Here and there you'd find a scrawny maple, or possibly a shrub. Geitner had one of the bigger and lusher campuses, replete with duck pond, weeping willows, and a six-story glass and brick office building.

Lennox started with the lobby but was barred from the elevators until she stated her business to the receptionist.

"I need to speak to Joan Strake," Lennox said.

"Regarding?"

Regarding Matilda Bauer. The receptionist rang up to Joan's office. Lennox waited. Turned out Ms. Strake was tied up in meetings through the rest of the week.

"I'm working with law enforcement trying to locate Matilda Bauer," Lennox said. "I only need a few minutes of Ms. Strake's time."

There was no getting around the receptionist. She took Lennox's phone number and company name. "I'll make sure she gets the message," she said, with not one crumb of encouragement in her voice.

So much for going through the front door. Lennox went back to her truck and drove to the back of the building looking for a telltale back door, a cement urn, or, if the gods of Geitner were benevolent, a shelter for the tobacco-addicted. Sure enough, on the northeast corner of the building were a windowless steel door and an empty brick planter. She'd just found the smoking section. She reached in her glove box and extracted a half pack of American Spirits and a disposable lighter.

Even in the rainy spring air, the back of the building stank like a six-foot long ashtray. She lit up. Held it between her fingers and watched it burn. Tobacco companies put chemicals in their cigarettes to make them burn whether you suck on them or not.

By the second cigarette, a skinny young man had come through the smokers' door, lighting up before the door had completely closed behind him. Lennox said hi. Said at her old job they gave smokers a real shelter with a roof. He nodded. A few flakes of dandruff shook loose and drifted onto the collar of his navy wool jacket. He asked her if she was new.

"Just started last Thursday. It's a temp position, but I heard maybe they might be able to use me up in Joan Strake's office."

The guy shrugged his bony shoulders. "Emily's always talking about what a good boss Strake is. Lets her take smoke breaks whenever she feels like it."

They small talked, the whole time Lennox weighing the merits of following him back into the building and going up to Joan's office or waiting outside for Emily. She was damp and dizzy from breathing all the nicotine, but it seemed a better bet to wait for Emily. The guy finished his cigarette and went back into the building.

It took another hour and three more cigarettes before a woman came outside. She smiled when she saw Lennox. It was one of those killer sweet smiles, like the kind some little kids give you, that makes you feel liked for no particular reason. She was plump, with a broad-cheeked face. Her flesh looked as soft and pale as bread dough.

She lit her cigarette. Her fingers were long and slender. She had an elaborate manicure, her nails pewter-colored with Hindu tracery decals carefully glued on top of each nail.

Lennox introduced herself.

The woman smiled again, the same way. "Emily Cross," she said.

Bingo. Here was someone who knew Matilda firsthand.

The breeze shook some rain off the eaves of the building.

"I just started as a temp in Human Resources," Lennox said. "They have me processing unemployment claims, mostly. Seems like a good place here."

"I like it," Emily said.

"You know my friend Matilda Bauer? She's the one got me the job."

Emily nodded and flicked the ash off her cigarette. "I work with her," she said.

"Yeah?" Lennox said. "I thought she mentioned a girl she works with. Would you tell her to call me? Down in H.R.?"

"She's not here today. She's sick."

"Again?" Lennox said. "She hasn't been here since I started. I tried calling her this weekend, but she didn't pick up."

Emily's whole demeanor shifted. She had her reservations about Matilda.

"Do you know what's wrong with her?" Lennox said.

Emily blew out a lungful of smoke. "I don't." Her face had become immobile. She probably had to do extra to keep up with Matilda's workload, so maybe she was just annoyed with Matilda, or maybe she flat didn't like her. However Emily felt, she wasn't going to confide in a stranger.

"I should call Rose, Matilda's mom," Lennox said. "See if she's okay."

"Maybe she'll be back at work tomorrow." Emily stubbed out her cigarette. "Nice to meet you," she said.

Lennox said, "Hey, where's a good place to go to lunch around here?"

Emily gave a little shake of the head, like her opinion was too humble to voice. "I like Samurai Bento," she said. And with a small wave of her hand, she turned to leave.

"Nice to meet you too," Lennox said to her back, and let it go at that.

Fulin was likely right—Matilda had left the state. The question being: why now? Lennox decided to try Matilda's house one more time before giving up.

CHAPTER 7

One last ditch try to locate Matilda. Lennox ordered the takeout from the bento joint Emily recommended and drove across town to North Portland. Emily wasn't crazy about Matilda. It was easy to guess why. All those sick days and Emily probably doing her work and Matilda's as well. Lennox would peg Emily as in her early twenties, but she already had that look like she was becoming invisible. And then there was Matilda, beautiful and manipulative. No one, not even invisible people, *especially* invisible people, like being taking advantage of.

Lennox climbed the Sunset freeway from the flatlands of the Silicon Forest back up into the Sylvan hills. At the crest of the hill, she looked down on Portland's skyline as it rose from the banks of the Willamette River. All these years, Lennox's whole life spent living here, and it was still a wonder sighting the city from the forest.

The rain let up for the moment. Semis threw up standing water on the road, and she needed her wipers again. Matilda would have to be clever to fool so many intelligent people, but just how far did her cleverness take her? Could she plan and execute long range? From what Lennox had seen of her files, Matilda had an elaborate network of people she was scamming, but she seemed reckless. Why else would she blow off her job and make an enemy of her parole officer?

It was one in the afternoon when Lennox parked along the curb outside the Bauer house, just on the remote chance that Matilda had returned home from wherever the hell she'd been. It was showdown time. Either she was here at the house, or she was irretrievably AWOL and Fulin would be forced to bench warrant her ass.

Rain dropped from the edge of Rose's stoop in big flat plops. Lennox pulled her neck into the collar of her jacket and rang the bell. She could hear the bell penetrate the house. It sounded deserted. No music, no sound of a television, no footsteps. She called Matilda's cell one last time.

She heard a faint ringtone. Lennox dialed again. It was coming from the front of the house. Lennox stepped off the stoop and backed over to the sidewalk to where she could see Matilda's dormer. The window was open four inches, the shade pulled to the bottom of the window. Lennox rang the doorbell again and pressed her face against the storm door, straining for any sound that suggested there was a person in the house. Nothing.

What was she going to do? She'd already stolen this woman's data and wiped her disk and now she was contemplating breaking into her house? She never would've considered this. Any of this. Less than two years ago, she'd been a cop. Now look at her, breaking and entering. Lennox didn't give herself justification, but reached into her bag and pulled out a pick. Jimmied the door. She unlocked the door at the knob, but it was dead-bolted further up.

She walked along the sidewalk to the back of the house, and found a lock she could pick without breaking it. Three minutes later, she was inside. Lennox wiped her wet shoes on the door rug and eased the door closed behind her. Rose's kitchen was painted white, with fifty-year-old Formica counters and white curtains that looked like they were freshly starched and hung. The quiet was unnerving.

Lennox walked through the kitchen through the dining room to the living room and called Matilda's cell once again. Matilda's phone could be heard plainly from her room.

Lennox slowly climbed the narrow stairs. There was a bad smell the closer Lennox got to the top of the steps.

And then Matilda.

Hanging from an eye hook anchored in the ceiling, a man's silk tie around her neck. The fingers of Matilda's right hand caught in the tie, trying to loosen it.

Fucking dead.

Lennox's heart hammered so hard in her chest she realized she was starting to hyperventilate. She needed to slow down, take it in slow. It was the shock. The house so quiet, and Matilda so dead.

A puddle of urine on the floor beneath Matilda's feet. Her white anklets stained yellow with it. The little bench from her childhood tipped on its side by her feet. A vibrator by the bench leg.

White anklets, black patent leather Mary Janes. A pleated schoolgirl skirt that didn't cover her pudendum. No panties. She was shaved. A white schoolgirl blouse unbuttoned to her waist. Her hair was done in long blonde pigtails and fastened with white ribbons.

The furnace turned on. A gust of air blew across the room from the partially opened window. Not enough breeze to turn the body. Lennox heard a car splash through the puddles outside, but it didn't penetrate the awful stillness of the room.

Matilda's face had turned gray and waxy. Her vacant eyes were bloodshot from the burst capillaries. The tip of her black tongue protruded from her lips; her face grimaced.

Lennox would give herself five minutes before she called the cops. The cops needed to be here before Matilda's mother came home.

She touched Matilda's arm. Her skin was cool and stiff from rigor mortis. Which would've meant Matilda had been dead around twenty-four hours. Of course with the window cracked, the body would've cooled at a faster rate. So Matilda may have come back to the house as early as noon on Sunday, but surely before Rose had come home from church. The horror was that Rose had come home some time in the afternoon Sunday not knowing her daughter was hanging from the ceiling upstairs. It was so quiet, and the smell turned Lennox's stomach.

From the knees down, Matilda's legs were purple-black from lividity. But Lennox would swear that there was more pronounced bruising than what the lividity suggested. She looked more closely. There seemed to be chafe marks. Scratches and bruising that could be the result of struggle.

Lennox examined the ligature. A silk tie tied in a granny knot. She had never run across a death by hanging and she wasn't a forensic expert. It appeared that Matilda's neck was not broken or dislocated. Lennox would guess that Matilda had died of strangulation.

The scene of the crime. Matilda's full-length mirror was positioned behind her. Dolls and teddy bears had been pulled from her shelves and repositioned around the base of the mirror. The body was angled facing Matilda's desk.

This whole thing looked staged. And if Lennox were to guess, the audience was on the internet. Had Matilda set up this charade, lost her balance, and died? But if so, where was the laptop? Why were her legs bruised and scratched? She had to have had a helper. Maybe a partner.

Or was there another way to view this? Possibly Matilda had set this up, and someone broke in, murdered her, and took the computer with him.

It had to be murder, though. This was murder.

Lennox had worked forty-three murders during her tenure with the Portland Police. Thirty-two shootings, six stabbing deaths, and five by blunt force trauma. Each one horrible in its own way. Most of the time what she'd witnessed was that the victim had gone into shock. Maybe they had an awareness of dying, maybe not. Just caught off guard and then gone before they knew what happened. Was it a mercy to be alive one minute, struck down the next? Like animals. Here. Gone.

Matilda's was a bad death. The struggle was all over her face, her neck, the hand that tried to loosen the man's tie that choked off her air. Panicked, struggling, never having dreamed that she could end up dead before she made thirty years old.

Does anybody deserve a bad death?

Lennox put her camera back into her bag and climbed down the stairs. Let herself out the back way and crawled back into the Bronco. Slammed the door and made the call to the cops.

CHAPTER 8

While Lennox waited for the squad car, she called Fulin. It went immediately to voicemail, and she didn't try to soften the message. Matilda Bauer had been murdered; Fulin would face questioning before the day was out.

Five minutes later, three cars pulled up. A squad car, the forensic guys, and bringing up the rear, the detectives in a black Crown Vic. Tommy Pavlik and his newest partner, a big redhead.

Eighty-eight detectives in the Bureau, and Lennox drew him.

Six months since she'd last seen Tommy. He'd been retreating down her porch steps, cursing her as best he could with a busted nose. Breaking that guy's nose had been one of the most satisfying moves of Lennox's life. He'd had her pinned beneath him, telling her he knew she wanted it. She had not wanted it. Before that, he'd broken her heart and ruined her career. And he was a shit detective on top of it, a man who cut corners and disappeared evidence.

She gave herself three deep breaths and stepped out

of the Bronco. Left her camera and notes in her bag on the floor of the truck and locked the door behind her. He'd get zip from her without a search warrant.

Tommy left his partner on the curb and crossed the street to her truck, stood right to her until they were toe to toe. She was forced to tip her chin up just to make eye contact. Past his nose, which was a little thicker, a little more bulbous, but not bad.

"You called this in?" he said. Saying it in that accusatory way of his. Like calling in the crime automatically singled her out as prime suspect.

"I did," she said.

"Where's the body?"

"Upstairs."

"How did you get in the house?" he said.

"The back door was unlocked."

He made a pissed off noise. "And you just walked in?"

Lennox shrugged.

"Had you been in the house before?"

"I was here Saturday and talked to Matilda's mother."

"Did you remove anything? Alter the scene in any way?"

"You've got some fucking nerve asking me that," she said in a low voice.

He stepped back and crossed the street to his partner. "Take her statement," he said.

The new partner's name was Craig Turner. Early thirties. Short ginger hair, red stubble rather than a beard. Close set, suspicious eyes.

It started raining again.

Lennox's official version: she was trying to find Matilda Bauer for a client. She wasn't able to reveal who the client was. She arrived at the Bauer residence at one p.m., called

Matilda's cell phone and heard the ringtone from inside the house. No one answered the door, so when she found the back door unlocked, she entered, went up to Matilda's bedroom, and found the body.

Craig Turner didn't ask her for her professional impressions. Craig Turner had the same general opinion that most cops have towards private detectives. Which is to say, a low one. She left him her address, landline, and cell phone number and was turned loose.

Lennox fired up the Bronco and tried Fulin again. Voicemail. "Play stupid," she said in the message.

What else was he going to do? Tell his supervisors he hired a private eye to track down his client? Not just any PI, but Lennox Cooper. This was such a train wreck, Lennox truly didn't know how Fulin could hang on to his career.

Lennox drove home. Called Fulin again with no result. She let herself into the house. It was still early afternoon. She opened the cupboard and poured herself a healthy glass of Cabernet and headed to her office.

Then opened the browser history on Matilda's computer. First the chat rooms: Matilda posing as an HIV victim, or as a woman who loved to be subdued, or to dominate. All different identities, all with Facebook friends and Twitter feeds. Something was here, something that connected Matilda to her murderer.

Two hours later, two glasses of wine, and further back into Matilda's browser history, Lennox found a site called Second Life. It sounded like a religious thing. But when Lennox booted the application, a comic book desert complete with saguaros, escarpments, and a good looking off-road truck filled the screen. But that's not what Lennox saw first. What caught her eye was a cartoon woman who looked exactly like the dead Matilda.

Same blonde pigtails and ribbons, same sexed-up school uniform; a tight white blouse and a plaid mini skirt so short Lennox could see her butt cheeks peeking out of her panties.

Lennox's heart knocked against her ribs until it hurt. This was seriously creepy, seeing the dead woman as a caricature.

But it was a lead. A solid lead. Once her heart settled down, excitement took over, the way only a good hand of cards or a real lead could.

The avatar's name was Tildy. Lennox had never been much of a gamer. In fact, the last game she even played was *Halo* with an old boyfriend from high school. Then she grew up and saw what real bullets do.

Lennox pulled her chair closer to her desk and chose the menu option to go to your last destination. Tildy stood in a school parking lot where there were a lot of sports cars and vintage cars with furry dice dangling from rearview mirrors. Adjacent to the parking lot was a lawn the color of a green crayon. A big stone sign read, 'Central High.' In the distance stood a two-story brick schoolhouse.

Lennox noticed two people having sex in one of the vintage cars. So where was the thrill in that? The girl's bare legs were visible from the car window, her feet probably braced against the roof of the car. Instead of furry dice, her panties dangled from the rearview mirror. Lennox tried to move her avatar to get a closer look.

The girl was naked except for her anklets. The boy was on top, humping the girl, his jeans gathered around his ankles. His muscles didn't flex or crease; the flesh didn't give. It looked a whole lot like her Ken doll doing Barbie back when Lennox was twelve.

There had to be more to this. Matilda wouldn't waste her time playing make-believe if she didn't have an angle.

She walked the Tildy avatar up to the school. A couple of kids stood at the corner of the building, smoking. They nodded at her.

Lennox scrolled through the help menu and found gestures. Made Tildy nod back. Lennox walked her avatar up to the front door of the building. The door wouldn't budge. She tapped the gestures button, then the help button. Nothing. Meanwhile Tildy stood by the front door like a dumbass.

Lennox posed the question on a wiki site. Discovered that double-clicking right would allow Lennox to control the avatar's hand, and then she could use the mouse directionally.

More kids were exiting the school. One of the boys looked over his shoulder at Tildy. Lennox couldn't tell if it was her lame moves or her skirt he was looking at.

Geez, Lennox was sweating. Already she was starting to identify with this Tildy chick.

Lennox got her avatar through the door. A long and deserted hallway stretched before her, flanked by gunmetal gray lockers. The banner tacked above the lockers read: "Go Tigers!" The whole deal brought back warm memories: watching football in the rain, her first homecoming dance, and her first grope. Sam Sussman—she hadn't thought of him in years. He was a nice kid.

Lennox turned the next corner. Eight girls, looking like Tildy, stood shivering in a line outside the principal's office. They looked more customized than the kids smoking by the front door of the school. Lennox scrolled down her gestures menu, found "shaking" and got behind a black girl with long beaded braids. The girls were different races, had different haircuts, and they all looked like schoolgirl strippers. A blonde girl ran out of the principal's office, sobbing. Her pleated skirt didn't cover half her butt cheeks. They were beet red. So she'd been spanked. On a virtual reality site.

The line moved up, and an avatar with long black hair closed the principal's door behind her.

"Hey, do you mind if I go next?" Tildy asked a frightened-looking redhead.

"I don't know if it's permitted," the redhead said.

Lennox wondered who these people were behind their avatars. Were they junior high kids that slipped past the age safeguards of the game or grown women living out some submission fantasy? Did they have husbands? Families? Were they stuck back in their high school days?

"Come on," Tildy said. "I'll tell him it's my fault I jumped the line."

"I'm not sure," said the redhead.

"Or I could tell him you put me up to it."

"No," said the redhead. "Please."

So much depended on how a person's pupils dilated or didn't. How the micro muscles around the nose or mouth tightened or grew slack. The cant of a body. So how was Lennox to know what the redhead really wanted behind those Barbie doll eyes?

The office door opened, and the brunette ran out. Her lips were swollen and her face tear-stained. Again with the red butt cheeks and what looked like switch marks.

"I know who you really are," Lennox told the redhead. The girl vanished.

Lennox walked Tildy through the door, fumbling as she tried to close it behind her. A tall, dark-haired man with a goatee stood in front of an enormous desk. His fly was unzipped, and he held a small whip. "I've been a very naughty girl," covered the blackboard behind his desk.

Tildy walked closer to him, taking little steps. Lennox realized she was a little scared of the guy. He watched her approach, then his image froze. It was as if the whole room froze. The image turned into little colored pixels. Lennox wondered if the program had crashed. Then the principal unfroze and leaned forward.

"Tildy?" he said.

"Yes," she said. "I've been a naughty girl."

"You're not Tildy." His eyes turned red. "Who the fuck are you?" he said.

How could this virtual man know who was behind the Tildy avatar? Did he know Matilda? Did he know she was dead?

Spit was flying from his mouth. He looked like the devil, and Lennox didn't even believe in the devil.

"Who are you?" he said. All caps, question marks and exclamation points.

Lennox panicked. She shut the browser down as fast as her fingers could move. And it was sayonara Second Life.

CHAPTER 9

The principal's office at Second Life's Central High was closed indefinitely. The line of little girls stood outside the office flicking their hair and staring at the office door with baleful eyes, but the door remained locked. Lennox checked the site day and night. It was getting to be compulsive.

Meanwhile, the notice for Matilda's funeral had been posted. Funerals are a great venue for homicide investigators, on account of eighty-two percent of the time, the murderer attends their victim's funeral. Crazy, but true. Nine out of ten times the victim is killed by someone she knew. Eighty-two percent was more than good enough to act on.

Lennox and Fulin sat in his BMW. Fulin's ride was quite the step up from her Bronco. But who would choose a car with a white leather interior? She could imagine her raspberry yogurt tipping over and staining the seat. The dashboard had a computer screen on her side. So many bells and whistles, it was hard to know if he was driving the car or playing a computer game.

They parked at the northwest corner of the church

parking lot under a rusty-needled tree. Lennox trained a long-range lens on the attendees as they left their cars and entered the church. Fulin recognized Matilda's cousin Sara, a plump blonde. The cousin helped Rose from the car, and they entered the side door. She also recognized Joan Strake, Matilda's boss, a tall, thin woman who shepherded Emily Cross and another woman into the church. It was pretty classy for her workmates to show up at the funeral.

"There's that sunuvabitch," Fulin said.

Lennox spotted Joey in a huddle of leather jackets, none of them looking like they'd seen the inside of a church in a couple of decades. They moved like a school of fish. Every so often one of the females reached forward and patted him on the back or squeezed his shoulder. Could any of these ladies have a motive for killing Matilda?

What about the other women in the church? "Do you know any of these people?" she said, pointing to a size zero with a pink crew cut. An old hippie woman.

Fulin shook his head.

"That one?" A skinny man in a Lincoln beard, black jeans, and a string tie. The hipster? The business dude who looked like a movie star playing a business dude? Could one of those guys be the Second Life principal? It would be taking a huge chance now that he knew someone was on to him.

Several groups of gray-hairs pulled into the lot in their Buicks, carrying either glass plates of cookies or some kind of covered casserole. Friends of Rose's, if Lennox were to guess. She took everyone's photo. The old people tottered to a side entrance that was likely a church basement.

A well-dressed woman in her late forties, wearing a tight black suit, was the last person to arrive. The woman bore a strong resemblance to her license photo. Debbie Paulson.

"I'm pretty sure that's the friend Matilda was spending the weekend with," Lennox said.

"She's a lot older than Matilda," Fulin said.

They waited in the car for ten more minutes. No one else showed up.

"Not many mourners," Lennox said.

Fulin asked if she was surprised. Guess not. She handed Fulin a miniature camera and told him to take a picture of every car in the lot, making sure he got a clear shot of the license plate.

"What are you going to do?" Fulin said.

"Watch the service. Watch for anyone who misbehaves."

"Do you figure anyone's really sorry she's dead?" Fulin said.

"Her mom," she said.

"I'll bet there's even a part of her that's relieved," Fulin said. "What about the guys she's swindled? You think they're going to show up here?"

"Early days," Lennox said. "We're casting a wide net."

His body sagged with resignation. "The cops are going to point to me on this one," he said.

"That's why we're working this," she said. "We're shining a light on anyone who might have had a reason to kill her."

Lennox left the car, eased the church door open, and slipped inside, her back against the wall. On a table by the door was a leftover stack of funeral notices. Lennox glanced at one. The prayer caught her eye. Psalm 4. "*In my distress you have set me at large; take pity on me and hear my prayer.*"

Poor Rose. Lennox sent up a prayer of her own that Rose could learn to block the memory of Matilda dressed like a hooker and remember her daughter as a child. Isn't there a time in all our lives when we're innocent and good? When all we want in life is to be safe and loved?

Lennox reached into her bag for her video camera glasses. If she pressed a button on the stem, they recorded everything she looked at.

A man came in and stood close to her. She knew who he was before she turned. She could smell him. His sweat, the smell of clover.

"Friend of the family?" he said in a loud whisper.

She pretended Tommy wasn't there, and eventually he went back to where he was sitting with his partner, Turner.

The organ led into the first hymn. A funeral is a funeral. Matilda's was no different from any other Lennox had gone to. Maybe less sniffling. The soloist began singing, "The Lord is my Shepherd."

She doubted that any of the grey-hairs in the congregation were responsible for Matilda's death. There was Joey and his buddies. There were the females behind them, who may or may not have been jealous of Matilda. There was Joan and Emily from work. There was Debbie, who appeared to be pulling tissues from her purse and pressing them up to her face. Crew-cut, Hipster, Movie Star and Lincoln sat solo towards the back of the church. The hippie woman sat next to Rose and the cousin.

Lennox was still sussing out the congregation when the minister walked to the pulpit, quoting from Psalm 4, "Children of men, how long will you be heavy of heart, why love what is vain and chase after illusions?" Matilda earned herself a PhD in illusions. How many people would she have robbed or ruined if she'd lived to Rose's age?

Joey stood up suddenly and pushed his way out of

the pew, his face red and furious-looking. She figured if he didn't find something to hit and soon he'd be bawling like a baby. He lurched towards where Lennox was sitting like he meant to haul her off, then he spotted Tommy and his partner and walked out.

What Joey didn't realize was that while Tommy may have taken an oath to protect and defend, it sure as hell didn't include her.

A few minutes later, Debbie slipped out. Her eyes and nose were red, her cheeks blotchy from crying. She put her head down and left as quickly as she could. Lennox thought maybe they weren't partners after all; maybe they were friends, pure and simple. If there was anything about Matilda that was pure and simple. Big questions being: how did they even come to know each other, and what could they possibly have in common?

Ten more minutes of congregational sniffing and psalms of solace, and the service was over. The reverend welcomed everyone down to the Apostles Room in the church basement. Rose and her relative left through the side door, and the rest of the assembled took their leave. Lennox stood against the wall and filmed everyone leaving the church. Then she turned off the power switch and returned her glasses to her bag.

Tommy Pavlik was waiting for her outside the church door.

"I could see you ending up some day like that Bauer chick," he said.

"I like your nose," she said. "Must've taken some work to straighten it."

Tommy took a step back like maybe she was going to break it for him again.

"C'mon Tommy," she said. "Lighten up."

"Isn't that Chen's BMW over there?" Tommy said. "He's your client isn't he?"

"You know I'm not going to answer that," she said.

"Like you're going to be able to save his ass." He started laughing. That laugh of his, full of mirth unless you knew him like she did.

CHAPTER 10

Lennox was the twentieth woman to join the Portland Police Bureau, but the first one to make detective. She remembered her first day, the all-hands meeting. Captain stood her up facing some seventy detectives, the only woman, so stick your chin up, give them an easy grin, and plenty of eye contact.

Sure, there were some wolf whistles, one of them coming from a tall stringy guy slouching in his chair. His legs stretched out in front of him, taking up more room than a body should. His laugh the same way, like it swept up every crumb of attention. You couldn't help but want to be in on the joke.

"John here has agreed to partner with Detective Cooper, show her the ropes," Captain said, nodding to a cop in his late forties.

"Wait a minute," Laughing Boy said. "No one asked me."

"No one trusts you," someone in the back said. More laughter.

"Watch out for that one," the captain said.

Laughing Boy was waiting outside the door for Lennox

after the all-hands. She felt a jolt of attraction and knew just as surely as his eyes were blue and his nose took a cute little turn to the left that he was trouble.

She'd always been attracted to bad boys. Why? The easy answer was that nice guys were predictable, and predictability bored her. Give her a problem, a secret, a guy who didn't want closeness, and she was all over him.

His name was Tommy Pavlik. And he invited her to the Lotus Room after shift. Lennox couldn't figure out whether he was including her in the gang or asking her out.

After shift, her partner drove home to his family, and Lennox drove to the Lotus Room. Tommy stood at the bar facing the door and waved to her the minute she stepped across the threshold, peeling himself from the other detectives so he could escort her back to the bar. His trophy, the lady detective. He introduced her to the guys. Bought her a drink, and the next one, too. His face crinkled in a perpetual grin that stretched to a laugh.

Some guys think they're the night's entertainment, but Tommy got just as much of a kick out of other guys' jokes. He made her giddy. Tommy was fine with the guys asking her about herself and making jokes, so long as they didn't get too friendly. "Hold on there," he said. "I saw her first."

Those guys all knew about Tommy. Knew that he was married. They weren't looking out for her. And you know what? She wasn't looking out for herself. She was still young enough back then to marry, have children, and make captain. Back then, she was young enough to have a good life.

By eight that night, the other guys had gone home, and Tommy asked her to dinner. They went to the Portland Grill on top of a glass office tower known as The Big Pink. The night sky stretched in all directions, the restaurant dark enough not to distract from the view, and through the glass the city lay beneath them, jewels, stars—twinkling like crazy.

They ate snails and shared a bottle of cabernet, Tommy giving her the skinny on how the department worked. Lennox asked him if he knew her partner, what the captain was like, who should she look out for. He kept it positive. He made her laugh.

It was just after ten when he walked her back to her car. It had stopped raining for the moment and the air smelled clean and cold. Bare trees rattled in the wind. He offered her his arm and she took it. A block from the Pink he pulled her closer to him, bent over, and smelled her hair. He moaned so low and soft it could have been wind. When they got to her car, he didn't try to kiss her or grope her. She thought maybe she'd been wrong about him, that maybe her luck had changed or maybe she had grown wiser somehow without noticing and now was ready for a meaningful relationship.

Two weeks later, her best friend, Ham, got wind of Tommy and her. Warned Lennox to stay the hell away. "He's married, he's got little kids."

Lennox told Ham, "We're just friends," like it was no big deal. Two weeks was plenty of time to begin thinking of him as something more than a friend. She confronted Tommy, and he gave her the same tired clichés you read in the advice columns any week of the year. "Can't we be friends?" he said.

Who were they kidding? Lennox knew all about guy friends. Wasn't she best man at Ham's wedding? The way she and Tommy were together had an altogether different energy. Just pals, just not. They stayed like that for a year, Tommy always pressing her for more. Then he told her he loved her. Told her they were soul mates. That night they drove to her house, and had sex on the dining room table.

CHAPTER 11

In less than a year and a half, Tommy had gone from lover to the subject of every "if only" fantasy to her enemy.

Tommy was on the television the next morning, announcing Matilda's murder on the Channel 4 News. Now that it was officially murder, Matilda's computer files were evidence. After the funeral, Lennox and Fulin had talked half the night about how to handle it. There was only one answer. Whether or not Tommy Pavlik ever used the data, it was evidence.

Turning over the external drive was going to sink Fulin. He decided to go to his boss and explain as best he could. Lennox would keep looking for the murderer until Fulin was out of the woods.

Along one wall of her office was a freshly scrubbed whiteboard. It was time to build a suspect list. Lennox taped Joey Tufts' photo on the "A" side of the board. His criminal record, her notes from her interview with him, and her interview with Rose all went into a file with his name on the label. Then she shuffled through her 5 × 7 photos from the funeral. Starting with the names in the funeral guestbook, she came up with driver license photos and matched them against the photos she'd taken at the funeral. She ruled out the baristas from the coffee shop close to Matilda's work, Matilda's cousin, and her aunts.

Two of the funeral attendees were Matilda's ex-boyfriends, although calling them boyfriends was a bit of a stretch. They were more like the scam du jour. Lennox pulled out a photo of the hipster guy. Jack Lutz appeared to be last year's boyfriend. Skinny black pants, geekoid glasses, and a fifties haircut, all very ironic. Lutz didn't have enough money to interest Matilda, but his parents did. It looked like Matilda had tried a couple moves on Mom and Dad with no success. Jack went on the "B" side of Lennox's whiteboard.

Next came the movie star, high tech guy. Boyish, square-jawed, dark hair falling over his brows. His name was Eric Thrasher, a high roller in high tech sales. He also was the boyfriend who pressed charges, resulting in her incarceration. Lennox checked the court records. Thrasher's wife divorced him the same year. Poor Mr. Thrasher ended up with half his original asset base, then got hit with a whopping spousal and child support.

That happened three years ago. Why would he go after Matilda now? Why not ask why it took so long for Lennox to splatter Tommy's nose across his face?

Lennox taped Thrasher's photo in the "A" column and put his data in a folder.

By three in the afternoon, Lennox had gotten to Matilda's boss, Joan Strake, and her coworker, Emily Cross. Why would Ms. Strake murder Matilda when she could simply fire her?

Lennox's phone blipped, and a text message came in

from Frank Cardo: "I'm in the neighborhood. U have time for coffee?"

She didn't have time.

Except when was a good time? And he was such a mensch. And cute. And he'd been understanding when she cut their dinner date short. He was a gentleman, meant with zero irony. If she wanted a boyfriend like she kept telling herself she did, then she needed to make some sort of effort. And a boyfriend would be good, on account of she hadn't been laid for seven—count them—seven months, which was a damned shame, her being in her sexual prime.

Lennox texted back, "Let's meet. Cup and Saucer? Ten minutes?"

Five of which were spent brushing her teeth, putting on lip gloss, and changing out of her gnarly old hoodie.

Rain sheeted down the big windows of the Cup. Frank sat by the last big window street side. He wore a navy sweater and blue shirt, looking post-preppy and pretty darned wonderful. His face broke into this wide, wide grin for her when he caught sight of her entering the place. She waved and ordered her coffee from a waitress with blonde dreadlocks.

"Hi there, stranger," she said.

"I blame that on you," he said.

"Fair enough." She couldn't tell him much about the case, but he'd seen the murder splashed all over the media. He smelled of cedar and oranges. He listened and asked smart questions. Then he asked her to dinner.

"Tonight?" she said.

Yes.

Yes.

Which was when her cell phone started chattering. A

text from Fulin: "I've been suspended."

It was what she'd feared. Would he have been suspended if she had left Matilda's laptop alone?

"I'm sorry, Frank. I have to make a call," she said.

"Sure," he said. But his face was anything but sure.

She left the table. One call turned into two. Lennox called Sarge to spread the word: all hands at the Shanty, as soon as they could get away. She'd go fetch Fulin.

Then she returned to the table.

"Fulin's been suspended. Ten years, and his career is over." Lennox shook her head. "I think they might even charge him with murder."

"I'm taking that you need to cancel our dinner," Frank said.

She reached across the table and took both of his hands in hers. They were broad and short-fingered, with callouses that surprised her, him being an accountant. It was a bold move, the first time they'd touched, so while she was being bold, she told him, "I like you. I'd like to get to know you better. I'm sorry this has happened just when we met." She released his hands. "It's kind of like you getting hit with a giant tax audit or something."

Frank's smile looked a little pained. "I get it. You don't need to put in context."

Great. She'd patronized him.

She left him sitting at the window table, with a shower of "Sorry, sorry, sorry," inside and a hard rain outside. So much for getting laid.

It continued to rain hard. Fulin sat on the steps of his condo, his hands clasped to his knees. When Lennox drove up to the curb in front of him, he didn't react. She rolled down the Bronco's window and called to him. Rain ran off

a blonde."

"What I don't get is why you even went online looking for love," Jerry said. "You had to know you were betting blind."

"You could've been dating a Nigerian guy. A robot," Ham said.

"Worse," Fish said. "A client."

Fulin knew better, but when you're lonely, you're more likely to take risks, and make mistakes. Sure, everyone knows that people pretend online. Like people don't pretend in real life? Take Frank. Lennox operated under the assumption that Frank was a decent, sweet guy. But he could have a wife and family somewhere. She could find out a year from now that he was an embezzler. Any time you take a chance on someone new, you're betting blind. It didn't matter whether it was online or face-to-face.

Fulin's head was bowed so low his forehead barely cleared the table. "After Lucy and I broke up, I thought I'd give a dating site a go. A lot of other people do it; I figured, hey, why not?"

"What I don't get," Fish said. "How come you didn't recognize her?"

"Airbrushing. Photoshopping. The woman I thought I was dating was mixed-race Japanese. I screwed up," Fulin said. "I should've come forward a month ago. Then it was murder and Lennox was holding all the data on her laptop. I had to go to the boss, turn over the external drive, try to explain myself."

Jerry pushed his scotch in front of Fulin, told him to drink, then turned to Lennox. The first time in ten years she'd seen him annoyed, and he was annoyed at her. "Your idea to download the woman's data. Wipe her hard drive?

Why?" he said.

"I tried to convince Fulin to go to his boss right from the get-go. Then I figured the next best thing was to find out what Matilda was up to. She had screen captures of Fulin masturbating. If she didn't have her data stored in the cloud, that would be the end of the blackmail."

Jerry and Fish wagged their heads at her.

But Sarge said, "I would've done the same."

"Not me," Fish said. "I would've told Chen go to his boss."

"You know what?" she said. "I told him that over and over. Go to your super. Explain things. He wouldn't do it."

"So you vandalized the chick's computer," Fish said.

"You're such a Catholic," Ham said to Fish.

Fulin said, "I figured even if I hung on to my job I'd be the biggest joke at the Bureau."

"Nobody's laughing," Ham said.

Sarge wore a navy watch cap over his bald head. His brows sank in disapproval. "So, you didn't go to the boss; you thought you'd have Lennox handle it."

Fulin quick looked around at the guys. "Who else?"

"Don't you see that hiring a PI just makes you look guilty?" Sarge said.

Katy, the cocktailer, cracked the door. "Refreshments, anybody?"

Jerry ordered a round of scotch. "Make them doubles, Katy."

"Bauer's mother claims Joey Tufts did the crime," Lennox said.

"We brought Tufts in for questioning," Fish said. "He claims Fulin threatened the victim. You're going to be looked at for the murder."

Fish said what Lennox had been afraid to say. Fulin had gone from a blackmail victim to a murder suspect.

"What kind of alibi does Tufts have?" Ham said.

"He was working all day with his boss," Fish said. "The boss verified it."

Ham shrugged. "Alibis can be faked. This Joey is a violent character. He could've found Matilda doing the nasty and lost it."

"Get yourself an attorney," Jerry said to Fulin. "A criminal attorney."

Kline. Kline was a good guy and the best criminal attorney in town. Lennox would call Kline tonight, wake him up if she had to.

They finally got around to what was on Matilda's laptop. Lennox told them about her big lead. The virtual high school. The guys didn't get it.

Jerry looked around the table and made eye contact with Sarge. Sarge nodded his head.

"Fulin," Jerry said. "This is going to hit the morning news."

"Sex scandal," Sarge said. He looked like it hurt him to say it.

Fulin stood up. He headed for the door, stumbling against Jerry's chair. He didn't close the door behind him.

Lennox got to her feet. Then Jerry stood up. "That's okay, Sherlock," he said. "I'll take him home."

CHAPTER 12

Lennox woke up to Cory Doran's fake blood splashed across her front door and puddled over her welcome mat. She stepped in it, the sticky syrup oozing between her toes. That fucking kid. That fucking fatherless kid. And who was to blame for that?

It's always easy to look back and see where you could've played the hand differently once all the cards are on the table. Same thing with Fulin. Sure, he should've gone to his supervisors a month ago when Matilda started messing with him. Maybe Fulin blew it when he hired Lennox to help find Matilda. But look what she'd learned about Matilda in four short days. Knowledge that Tommy Pavlik was never going to unearth even with all of Matilda's data. She could solve this murder and prove Fulin's innocence. Starting with Joey Tufts' alibi.

Lennox found Joey's boss coming out of the outdoor toilet set on the curb in front of a large Spanish villa on the Alameda. The Alameda was a northeast street that wound along the ridge carved out by Lake Missoula in the last

Ice Age. Very pricey on account of it had a great view of downtown Portland rising out of the trees, and the West Hills beyond. It was nine in the morning and not raining at the moment. The air smelled of wet cement. The crew was tearing off old stucco, which had no doubt rotted. The boss's name was John Hill, owner of Hill Construction. He specialized in classic home remodels, according to his web site. He had a DUI twelve years ago; otherwise he was clean. His wife Mary ran his office, and a small accounting service handled their taxes. Joey had been working for him since his release a year and a half ago. Hill was Joey's alibi.

"Mr. Hill?" Lennox said.

Hill looked down at her from a great height. She'd peg him at six foot three and skinny as a crane.

Lennox waved her license at Hill and asked if she could have just five minutes of his time. He looked over at his crew. They were standing on scaffolding, tearing off the stucco with crowbars.

"What about, exactly?" John said over the noise of the pounding and the dropping cement.

"On Sunday, March 5th, you told the police that Joey Tufts was working for you from eight in the morning until four thirty that afternoon."

"That's right." John Hill glanced again at his crew. Lennox looked up and saw Joey standing on the scaffolding, a crowbar in his hand. She smiled and waved at him.

"Were you working on this project?" Lennox asked.

John shuffled his weight from foot to foot. There was something about weekends that could make a small business owner twitchy.

"No. It was a garage reroof," he said.

"Were you working as well?"

"Yeah, Joey and me. We did the teardown, resheathed and shingled it."

"Would you mind giving me the address?" she said. "And maybe showing me the paperwork? Just for my records."

Hill looked truly alarmed. Obviously Detective Pavlik hadn't asked him for this level of verification. And Lennox had a strong hunch the job, if there was a job, was not on the books.

"Well, I don't know if I can show you that," he said. He continued to rock from foot to foot on his skinny bird legs. The sky darkened and the air smelled like rain.

"You know," she said. "Just the entry for the work. And Joey's payroll information for that date? That's it. I won't have to bother you again."

"We've been very busy this last month," Hill said. "I'm not sure my wife's caught up with the paperwork."

"It gets more complicated," she said. "If our attorney needs to subpoena your records." Which was total horseshit. Fulin hadn't even been charged yet, much less hired an attorney.

Hill paled. Maybe she'd get more cooperation if she dialed it back a little. She told him she understood, the books were always the last thing to get done when you were busy. She gave him until the end of the week to produce his paperwork, and watched him squirm.

So much for Joey's cast iron alibi.

CHAPTER 13

Cruising through Matilda's data, Lennox started with the men Matilda designated "active customers." Twenty in all, twelve of them easily tied to Matilda's plea of "I need money, please help." Those twelve guys continued to email her, ask her where she was and why she hadn't written. Lennox put them aside for now. It was the remaining eight that needed a closer look.

What if one of these eight men was the spanking principal? Say Matilda met him in Second Life and at some point coaxed him to meet her in the flesh. What if she got him to act out his fantasies in reality, then blackmailed his ass?

It was a good theory. The murdered Matilda had been dressed in the same little girl clothes as her avatar. And how had the Second Life principal known that the person manipulating Tildy, Matilda's avatar, was not Matilda? He knew because he'd killed the real Matilda.

What could Lennox reasonably guess about this dude? Statistically there was a certain kind of person who got a kick out of spanking: male, and probably middle-aged or older. Color him white.

Lennox did a deep search on the eight men. They all fit the profile, and each had made a four-figure down payment to Matilda, with a three-month lapse, then a three-figure monthly payment. It looked like a blackmail scheme to Lennox, but what Matilda had on these guys was buried deep enough that Lennox hadn't been able to find it. What she did find was that of the eight men, five lived out of town and had not flown to Portland in the calendar year. The remaining three lived locally. Matilda had squeezed some serious money from all three. Each of them must've had something to hide.

The very best candidate was Hobby Glover, vice principal at Cedar Hills High School. Surrounded by teenaged girls, some of them still children, some of them giving a credible semblance of womanhood. Glover was white, forty-nine years old, married, no children. His DMV picture showed a plump, bespectacled man, not at all the kind of tough guy you usually see as a vice principal. Was there steel in those eyes? She couldn't tell in the photo, but she was dying to meet him. A search engine yielded the names of the student body of Cedar Hills. Lennox called the school posing as Charlotte Lake, a freshman's parent, but she was told that there must've been a scheduling mistake. Mr. and Mrs. Glover were whale watching down at Yaquina Bay and weren't coming home until the end of spring break.

On to the second candidate: Phillip Juelly, single, aged fifty-three. Phillip had worked in the rare books room at Powell's for the last fifteen years. It was Phil who had located the uncut first edition of Biddle's history of the Lewis and Clark expedition. Phil was on Facebook. He wore a black shirt and had a neat little mustache beneath a prominent nose. His smile showed no teeth. His Facebook profile gave him forty-two friends, most of them from Powell's, a few from the Oregon Historical Society, and a sprinkling of family. Lennox spent some serious time tracking down each of his friends, but she didn't find Matilda in any of her disguises. Had Phillip unfriended her?

Lennox called Powell's and found out that Phil finished his shift at eight p.m. She could confront Mr. Juelly, ask him if he spanked little girls online. Ask him if he killed Matilda. And he would deny all of it. Confront him looking like Matilda in her naughty girl costume and Lennox might get an altogether different reaction.

She went upstairs and pulled her jeans and socks off. Changed her undies to white. In the back of her closet was a navy and green plaid pleated skirt resembling a school uniform. Back when she was in vice, she'd found it at a resale shop. She had cut the bottom half off the skirt and rehemmed it so that it barely covered her butt. The dark plaid made her legs look white as school paste. She couldn't go out in public with those thighs.

Of course she could. She took a deep breath and buttoned the white school blouse. White anklets and black Mary Janes completed the uniform. She caught her hair up in two long pigtails and tied them in white ribbons.

If you put a silk tie around her neck, she could've been Matilda at the crime scene. Matilda with dark hair and thicker thighs.

She pulled a pair of sweats over the skirt and slipped into her leather jacket. Drove down Burnside, past clapboard churches, row houses, empty lots with yellow grass, past Hippo Hardware, then crossed the Burnside Bridge. The cherry trees lining the river south of the bridge had paled from pink to white in the late twilight.

She drove through Old Town, where the drunks sat on the wet sidewalk, their backs against the historic brick buildings, their heads lolling against their chests. Young hipsters stepped over the drunks' legs to get into the nightclubs. The live music would start in an hour. By then the drunks would mostly be passed out. Old Town had been Old Town since Lennox could remember. Hell, at one time Lennox herself had been a youngster climbing over some passed out dude to get to the bar.

She parked on the street four blocks down the hill from Powell's, swung her legs out of the truck, and wiggled out of her sweatpants.

Powell's City of Books stood near the top of the first hill climbing up to the West Hills. Taking up the entire block, the store had a glass front, its marquee lit red and white and announcing a *New York Times* bestselling author arriving Thursday at seven. Beneath the marquee, a large porch that could comfortably shelter thirty people and fifteen bikes. A twenty-year-old boy and girl in batiked rags and yellow dreadlocks sat partially blocking the entrance. They held cardboard signs asking for money. Lennox felt them staring at her white legs as she stepped onto the porch. A middle-aged man left the store with a canvas bag full of books. Two teenaged girls and an Asian boy stood by the bike racks. The girls had dyed black hair, the boy blond. All three wore eyeliner; all three were smoking. The girls sneered at Lennox; the boy giggled; smoke seeping from their curled lips.

Embarrassing. The one piece of fortune was it was unlikely that Lennox would run into anyone she knew. Her tribe wasn't big on reading. She tilted her chin up, thought fuck those little kids, pulled a cherry Tootsie Pop from her bag, unwrapped it, and put it in her mouth.

"Isn't she like thirty?" said one of the smokers to the other.

Like thirty. Bless her little heart. Lennox kept the Tootsie Pop in one cheek and leaned against Powell's front window, waiting for Phillip Juelly to exit the building. Lennox heard techno music from a club nearby. The wind picked up from the north and west, bringing with it a faint smell of boiling malt from a microbrewery down the street.

At 8:17, Phillip walked out the door. He was a hunched, six-foot-two, shambling version of his Facebook self. Wrinkled khaki trousers, a corduroy jacket with a raveled edge, a black shirt buttoned to the top button.

Lennox overtook him before Phillip had a chance to know what was happening. She grabbed his sleeve to halt him, took a theatrical lick from her Tootsie Pop, and said in a baby-doll voice, "I'm sorry, teacher, I've been a very naughty girl."

He looked at her with the blank look of a person who'd just seen his first alien. The truth was as clear as a crystal spring in March: this dude was not a spanker of young girls, really or virtually. He put his hand up to shield his sight from her, his face flushing deep red. He looked back at the front door of the store in a panic.

"I'm sorry," she said. "It was a mistake. Are you okay?"

"Who are you?" he said. He looked mad and ready to have a heart attack all at the same time. "My ex put you up to this, didn't she?"

Lennox got that old familiar feeling she was going to be detained. How many times had she been manhandled since she turned PI? The last thing she wanted was Juelly grabbing her and calling the cops. Trying to explain why she looked like a hooker to a cop who may or may not know her. Or like her. Lennox told Juelly sorry one more time, then sprinted up the block.

"You tell her, she'll never get a dime from me," he shouted after Lennox.

The one thing you can say about short skirts is there's freedom of movement. It was dark and damp, and the wind was blowing harder. Four cars honked at her, three of their drivers catcalling from opened windows. She caught the walk sign at the next corner and didn't look back until she reached the Bronco. She unlocked the door and jumped in.

Most people find it awkward to pull on a pair of sweatpants behind the wheel of their rig. It's all a matter of motivation.

Lennox thought about Phil Juelly on her way home. Maybe he wasn't a spanker of little girls, but he was somebody worthy of blackmail. The rain turned hard. She flipped the wipers on high as she drove across the Burnside Bridge. It was raining in buckets by the time she pulled into the driveway. She made a run for the house and let herself in, the rain beating on her porch roof.

She moved through the house turning on lights, toweling her hair dry, and putting the kettle on for tea, then walked into her office.

The minute she went through the door, the man was on her. He came up from behind the door and held her neck in the crook of his arm, lifting her off the floor. She kicked, her feet trying to reach the floor. She was choking.

"You think you can fuck with me? A little runt like you?" he said. The voice was gravelly and familiar. His smell was familiar too: drugstore aftershave with a tang of sweat. Joey Tufts.

Hammerlock. Broken neck; asphyxiation. Dying like Matilda. Lennox lifted herself on her assailant's arm like she was going for a pull-up to keep herself conscious and dug her nails into his arm.

He released her and shoved her hard against the desk. Her screen fell over and made an ugly cracking sound. She rolled off the desk. Her keyboard crashed to the floor, and she landed on her feet before you could say "assault." Old Ugly, her service revolver, was loaded and nestled next to her paperclips in the top drawer of her desk. She dove for the drawer.

He dove for her. Joey Tufts. He yanked her arm back and she half spun and kicked him with every bit of training and force she had. And nailed him right where she was aiming. He crumbled, moaning. She grabbed her revolver from the desk drawer and moved away from him until her back was against the wall, her legs planted apart, the gun trained on his body. The adrenaline rush, the vanquished attacker; she still had the goods.

It took Joey five minutes before he could stand straight. By the look of him, she didn't have much hope for any cooperation, but she'd give it a try.

"Fuck you," he said. He pushed past her to get to the door. She had to hand it to him; the guy had guts.

She clicked the safety off Old Ugly. Joey was familiar with the sound, and it was enough to stop him cold.

"I can shoot you, say I was protecting myself," she said.

"Go ahead, I'm out of here." He moved down the hall towards the living room.

She took aim and shot the wall a foot from his ear. The

damage to her plaster was worth it. He screamed and hit the floor, his hand covering the side of his face.

"Holy shit," he cried. "What is wrong with you?"

"I want answers," she said.

"You want to pin Mattie's murder on me. I saw you talking to my boss. I saw your fucking suspect list."

"I don't know everything about the autopsy," she said. "But what I've heard was that there were no marks on Matilda that indicated that she struggled before she was hanged. Somebody coaxed her into dressing the way she did, putting that ligature around her neck."

"The Chink."

He made a move towards her. She told him, "Steady."

"She fucked with people, you know?" he said. "It wasn't for real."

"What people?" Lennox asked.

"People on the internet. Stupid people."

"But someone real pushed her off that bench," Lennox said. "Held her by the legs until she strangled. That wasn't some internet person."

"Don't look at me. I've got an alibi."

"This is bullshit," she said. "You supposedly knew Mattie better than anybody and you haven't given me squat. Tell me something I don't know or I'm calling the cops."

It was the same look she'd seen hundreds of times at the poker table when she called someone's bluff. Surrender. Truculent, sure, but surrender.

"Mattie had a friend. If you knew Mattie, you'd know how weird that was. She didn't hang with women even when we were in school."

"What's this friend's name?"

"Debbie."

"What about her? Was she a partner, a lover? What?"

"Mattie wouldn't talk about her. Said they were just friends. I figured Mattie was fucking her. Playing the woman, which made sense. This Debbie chick ran a dating service."

"Could Debbie have been Matilda's partner?" Lennox said.

"I don't know nothing about partners," Joey said. "Mattie was the kind of girl who worked alone."

"Was she good with computers?"

"Maybe. I don't know," he said. "She could've learned some stuff at work."

Lennox stepped back and lowered her gun. Joey got to his feet and brushed the plaster dust off his jacket. Lennox followed him through the front door, gun in hand. He hustled down the porch steps and didn't look back. Once he reached the driveway, he shot his arm up and gave her the bird.

CHAPTER 14

Two hours of data mining yielded an in-depth profile on Debbie Paulson. She was fifty-three, married to her college sweetheart, Al. There was information about their income, their children, and their house: a 4,600-square-foot ranch on the Willamette River. Zillow.com pegged the property at $2.5 million. Debbie had made the Sunday Living section of *The Oregonian* last September as an honest-to-God matchmaker. Debbie's business was called Simpatico. Slogan: *Welcoming Love Into Your Life*.

What to make of a friendship between a twenty-eight-year-old woman who preyed on lonely hearts, and a fifty-three-year-old matchmaker? What could they possibly have in common other than business?

Lennox made the call to Simpatico for her personal consultation. As soon as possible, Lennox said.

"We could see you at two this afternoon," the receptionist said in a low, whispery voice.

Lennox fished through her false identities and chose Molly McCarthy, tax attorney. Twelve years of dinner parties with Ham and his wife Meghan, who was a bona-fide tax attorney, gave Lennox enough legal-accountant-speak to fake it.

At one thirty she left the office and drove to John's Landing, a narrow stretch of river land just south of the downtown district. Simpatico was nestled in an office suite in the Water Tower Building. Red carpet, framed photos of happy couples young and old, a red metal heart hanging from behind the receptionist's desk. Next to the heart in metal script, Lennox read: "Find love, enjoy love, keep love."

"What's your success rate?" Lennox asked the receptionist, Madison.

"Seventy-four percent." The receptionist discreetly studied Lennox's tailored trousers and turquoise silk blouse, judging her with her twenty-year-old eyes. We're all swimmers in the river of time, Lennox thought. Just you wait, sister. Spending your days anticipating when you'll see your lover, anticipating your next paycheck, next party, next episode of blah blah blah—and poof! You're thirty-nine and wondering where the hell the time went.

Lennox handed over her fake picture ID to the girl. Then she sat down to sign the release forms and fill out the self-assessment, starting with the expected data about residence, employment, general health, and dating history. Lennox's dating history was cringe-worthy: a seven-month drought before a string of one-nighters, before a murder suspect, before a married man. Lennox figured what the hell, maybe this Debbie person had some insights she could pass on to Molly McCarthy.

Finally, she was ushered into Debbie Paulson's office. Soft colors, soft light, everything keyed to revealing dreams, telling secrets to the nice older lady behind the desk.

Only instead of the nice older lady, there was her twenty-something assistant named Nicky. Nicky offered Lennox herbal tea and perused Lennox's self-assessment.

"Where's Debbie?" Lennox said.

"She's not in today," Nicky said. "So Molly, tell me about your romantic goals."

"I really wanted to see Debbie. Could I reschedule?"

Turned out Debbie was out on personal time, and Nicky had no idea when Debbie planned on returning. Just from the look on Nicky's face, it was obvious that she was unhappy that her boss had gone AWOL.

Lennox said, "That sounds serious."

Personal time. Debbie looked pretty broken up at the funeral. Did her taking personal time have something to do with Matilda's death?

"I see you've listed a lot of men in your dating history," Nicky said. "Why do you think that is?"

"I'm sorry, Nicky, but I can't take relationship advice from someone a decade younger than me," Lennox said. "I'll come back when Debbie is here."

"When it comes to love," Nicky inquired, "do you have the time?"

Okay, that hurt. But back to work. She returned to the Bronco and drove ten miles to Debbie and Al's oversized ranch on the river.

Tall and bosomy, Debbie met Lennox at the door. The smell of cleaning products nearly knocked Lennox off her feet. It was like a battle between ammonia and lemon-scented disinfectant. So far, the ammonia was winning. Odd that Debbie was cleaning her own house.

She was dressed in a loose denim shirt, tight jeans, and yellow rubber gloves. Only a thin margin of blue surrounded her pupils. Debbie was high, which was probably why she was on a cleaning jag. Drugs could have that effect. Once Ham had found his wife, high on post-surgical drugs, cleaning the bathroom grout with a toothbrush at three in the morning.

"I'm ill," Debbie said. "You'll have to come back later."

Lennox showed Debbie her license. "I just have a few questions about Matilda Bauer," she said. "It will only take a minute of your time."

It's funny how a license has this magic effect on people. How they believe you're a person of authority even when you're not. Criminals, like Joey Tufts, know better.

Debbie's hands shook as she peeled off the rubber gloves, still reeking of ammonia, and clutched them in her hand like a limp bouquet.

She escorted Lennox into the living room, where the smell wasn't quite as strong. The room was painted a pale peach, the furniture upholstered in a bold floral.

Debbie twisted the gloves in her lap and looked at Lennox anxiously. Lennox sat opposite her, explaining she was investigating Matilda's murder. "You were with Matilda Saturday, March 4th, and she was murdered the next morning," Lennox said. "You probably were the last person to have seen Matilda Bauer alive."

"No," Debbie said. Her head wagged side to side like a dog with something in its ear. What the hell kind of drug was she on?

"Then who?" Lennox said.

"The murderer."

"Do you have any ideas who that might be?" Lennox said.

Debbie shook her head and pressed her lips together

tightly. Her eyes filled with tears. "Excuse me," she said, and fled the room.

Three minutes later, Debbie returned looking just as teary and just as drugged. She'd probably scarfed down another pill.

Lennox waited until she was reseated, and then told her not to worry, this was just routine. Where was she on Sunday the 5th?

The question penetrated Debbie's drug haze. She seemed to realize that she, Debbie Paulson, could be implicated in Matilda's death.

"Maybe I should get a lawyer."

"It's just a simple question," Lennox said. "I didn't mean to alarm you. But if you wish to talk it over with your husband, I understand."

That's right, sister, if you're going to lawyer up, you're going to have to tell the hubbie. The longer it took Debbie to decide, the more it looked like she was harboring a big, fat secret.

"Al and I went to church," she said. "We stopped for breakfast in West Linn, then Al went to the shop, and I started a roast and worked on the books all afternoon."

"Any witnesses?"

Debbie shook her head.

"Tell me about Matilda's business," Lennox said.

Debbie looked truly puzzled. "She worked as a secretary," she said.

"Not her straight job, her real job," Lennox said.

"I don't know what you mean." And damn if she didn't look convincing. Maybe it was time to take another tack.

"Her real job," Lennox said. "Her real job. Like Simpatico. Preying off lonely hearts."

Debbie jumped to her feet and stood towering over Lennox. "Simpatico helps people. We have a success rate of seventy-four percent. You don't even know what I do." Debbie was so indignant, she forgot she was frightened and in tears.

"So you're legitimate," Lennox said.

"Of course I'm legitimate," Debbie said. "You can't come into my home and tell me I'm some kind of shyster."

"Okay. I believe you," Lennox said. "But, don't you think it's suspect that your clientele were the same folks Matilda was scamming?"

"Mattie was a secretary," Debbie said.

"You weren't partners?" Lennox said.

"Of course not. I've built this business over the last twenty-three years."

Debbie still seemed outraged, but there was something else there. So far Lennox believed ninety percent of her story, but this last denial had a hint of untruth.

"Then partners in what?"

Debbie shook her head.

"What was your relationship?" Lennox said.

Debbie slumped back to the other end of the sofa.

"Friends," Debbie said. Lennox wasn't buying it.

"Tell me about your friendship," Lennox said. "You're in your fifties, well-known in the community; you have grown children, and Matilda was a convicted felon, still in her twenties. How did you even meet her?"

"She came to Simpatico looking for a husband."

Now that, Lennox could believe.

"She didn't have much in the way of a career, but she was very charming and comported herself well. I would never have believed that she grew up in foster care."

"Don't believe it," Lennox said. "She was living with her mother right up until her murder."

"Her parents were drug addicts. The state took her away when she was six."

Lennox shook her head. Debbie wasn't selling it.

"That's how she got in trouble," Debbie said. Maybe that was the first story Matilda told Debbie. But Debbie had learned the truth somewhere along the line.

"You were at the funeral," Lennox said. "You saw her mother. You saw all the photos of Mattie with her parents. Did that look like a drug-addled childhood?"

Debbie started to cry.

"Mattie lied to people, robbed them, blackmailed them," Lennox said. "That's who she was."

Debbie buried her head in her hands and sobbed. Big, theatrical sobs. "I don't feel at all well," she said. "You'll have to come back later."

Lennox let herself out, and headed back to town. Debbie's alibi was shaky, plus her business dovetailed with Matilda's scams, making Debbie definitely an A-list suspect. But look how passionately she'd jumped to Matilda's defense. Passion. Hadn't Joey said he figured Matilda was fucking Debbie?

And had Debbie's husband been simpatico with his wife's friendship with Matilda? Lennox would go to the horse's mouth for the answer.

CHAPTER 15

Spring break ended, and Hobby Glover, the vice principal at Cedar Hills High School, was back at work. Lennox couldn't let go of the coincidences between Matilda's avatar, Tildy, and Matilda. There also was a clear record of Matilda getting money from Glover.

After the disaster with Phil Juelly, it took fortitude to wiggle back into her schoolgirl uniform and put her hair in pigtails. But it's straight out of freshman psychology class, how the pupils dilate when the body likes something. The Chinese figured that out hundreds of years ago when dealing jade. Plus there's the way all the facial muscles soften and get mushy. Who knows, maybe the body gives off a scent that only the hindbrain picks up. Anyone paying attention gets it. Maybe they know squat about Chinese jade dealers; maybe they can't analyze it; but they get it.

If he was turned on by her little girl act, along with the blackmail he paid to Matilda, then dollars to donuts he was Second Life's spanking principal.

Lennox pulled into the school parking lot just as school

let out. She watched all the teenagers load into school buses or drive away in their daddies' cars. Twenty minutes later the parking lot was emptied. Another forty minutes dragged by. Lennox's eyes were glued on the side door closest to Hobby's car, a late model Subaru wagon.

About the time Lennox was wondering what to have for dinner, out stepped Hobby Glover. A Humpty Dumpty physique, thick wavy hair that didn't go with his plump little face. Glasses. You had to think the kids made fun of this guy. Lennox unwrapped a Tootsie Pop, this one orange for good luck, and hopped out of her truck.

"Mr. Glover?"

His pupils dilated.

Bingo.

"I'm Tildy," she said. "From Central High?"

The air crackled with his arousal, before it shifted to horror.

He leaned against his car and jerked his head from the school to the parking lot, looking for witnesses. He breathed hard for a few seconds, then he said, "You're not Tildy. I'm calling the police."

He reached into his hip pocket for his cell phone.

She reached into her bag and waved her license at him.

"You'll probably get Gregory Bartel in vice," she said. "We call him Fish. You can tell him all about Second Life and how you know that I'm not Tildy."

The hand stayed in his pocket. "I don't know what you're talking about," he said. Which was why he turned pale and sweaty-looking.

"Come on Glover, you knew her. Tell me her name."

He shook his head.

"C'mon dude," she said. "It's all there in her data files.

She was blackmailing you. Say it. Say her name."

Hobby Glover pulled the cell phone from his pocket. He fumbled the phone, and it fell to the pavement. One of the phone's doors broke off and its batteries popped out. He bent to retrieve the parts and came up red-faced. He was so busted. The question now being: was he only a blackmail victim, or a murderer?

"Matilda Bauer," he said.

"Last year you paid Matilda $5,300," she said. "Tell me why, and I'm out of here."

"I don't know what you're talking about." Glover stuffed the pieces of his broken phone back in his pocket. "What do you want from me?"

"I know Matilda was a bad person. She tricked people, got them in trouble, blackmailed them. What happened to her, she probably had it coming."

"If you had any proof, you wouldn't be here on this fishing expedition." Glover glanced at Lennox's thighs and refocused his gaze eyeball-to-eyeball. He kept his hand in his pocket, jiggling the phone parts.

Then he said her name, Lennox Cooper. Said it like he had something on her he could use. But what could he do? Report her? He'd have to reveal the reason she'd approached him. Go after her? She'd kick his ass.

Then he grinned, a sneaky little shit grin. Unlocked his car, Mr. Casual. Then he drove over the curb.

Sure as sure Glover was the spanking principal. And he didn't deny playing principal on Second Life and he didn't deny being blackmailed. Those two things, plus Matilda being dressed at the crime scene exactly like her avatar, made Hobby Glover the lead suspect.

Next step? Visit Mrs. Glover, find out what Hobby was

doing on March 5th.

And let's hear it for dressing up like a tart. She debated stopping at Cyril's for a nice bottle of red to celebrate, but decided it was better to change first.

When Lennox pulled into her driveway, Frank waved from her porch steps. He was dressed in good slacks and a fresh shirt. His dark hair was still wet from the shower. She bet he smelled great. She watched his expression change when she locked the truck and walked towards him. He went from glad-to-see-you to terribly confused in less time than it takes to wipe a smile off your face.

She pulled out the pigtails and fluffed her hair. "I was undercover," she said. "For work?"

"I figured I'd just show up, maybe go to dinner?"

It was like he was tripping on his own tongue. She seemed to always knock him sideways. She was a far cry from the accountant, lawyerly set he usually hung with. He didn't get her, but she could tell he wanted to.

She had planned on working. She was always working.

"Can you give me a minute to change?" she said.

She told him to make himself at home and went upstairs. She stripped down to her white undies. Then took off those, too, and changed into her best black lace underwire and matching panties, the kind of underwear she'd want to be seen in if she was taking off her clothes. What was she thinking? She was thinking she liked this guy. She was thinking, when it came to love, did she have the time?

CHAPTER 16

Frank was a mild mannered tax guy, but in bed Lennox had gotten her books balanced and then some. Proving you can't tell how it's going to be when two bodies get together. Frank was different from the guys she'd been with. He wasn't an edgy bad boy that anyone with a crumb of sense wouldn't consider having a relationship with.

Was that what she was doing here in Frank's bed? Looking for a relationship?

It was a nice bed. In a nice old house with lath and plaster walls and cove ceilings. Nice neighborhood, too.

Maybe she was finally learning from her past disasters. Maybe she was growing up. The smell of brown butter wafted down the hallway. She helped herself to a white T-shirt from Frank's bureau and slipped back into her black lace panties, then grabbed her cell phone and went to investigate.

Frank was frying thick slices of bread with an egg nested in the center of each slice. Damn! Someone should've told her that learning from past mistakes came with breakfast.

He gave her a big smoochy kiss. His mouth was fresh and tasted of peppermint. "The coffee's over there." He nodded in the direction of the counter beside the stove. "Would you get the papers?"

Lennox loved this. Waking up with the man you had sex with. Good sex, too. And having breakfast like married people. She opened the front door to a cool breeze blowing east along Farley Street. The cherry trees planted on the avenue shed pink blossoms across the sidewalk. She scooped up the *The New York Times, The Wall Street Journal,* and *The Oregonian.*

Sure enough, Matilda made the lead story in the Metro section: *Bauer death ruled homicide. Sources say murder possibly linked to Portland Police.*

She scanned the rest of the article. The victim was twenty-eight. Two men were being questioned at this time. So that would mean Joey Tufts and Fulin Chen. Frank was sliding fried bread onto two plates.

"Smells great," she said.

"Would you like juice or anything?" he said.

"The Bauer murder," she said. "It's splashed all over the media."

"Really?" he said. "Couldn't we just have breakfast?"

She told him how important it was. Phone in hand, she speed surfed through the network news shows.

"What do you say to dinner tonight?" Frank said. "There's a great little place in the neighborhood."

"I'd love to, but I've gotta work." Lennox didn't even want to think how Fulin was taking all this. What his must-save-face parents must be thinking.

"How do you know Fulin isn't guilty?" Frank said. "He hires you before he's even been charged with anything. He falsifies her paperwork, gets in a fight with her boyfriend."

"I know him. He didn't do it."

Frank looked at her untouched plate, the egg congealed.

"I'm going to take a shower," he said.

She called Fulin. Once he answered, she didn't want to bring up the fact that he was implicated in Matilda's murder. "Where are you?" she said.

"At your office," he said. "Where are you?"

"I got laid last night," she said in a low voice.

"I'll be lucky if I ever get laid again," Fulin said in a glum voice. "I've got an appointment at nine with August Kline. What do you want me to do before that? "

She told him to get started on Emily Cross' and Joan Strake's history. Everything. Credit, criminal, families and friends.

She was on the phone with Fulin when Frank walked back into the kitchen dressed for work. He stood in front of her chair looking disappointed in her.

"I'll call you back," she told Fulin.

She turned off the phone and told Frank she was sorry. "It's just that Chen is this close to being indicted."

"I have to go to work," he said.

Jeez. All she had on was panties and his tee shirt. "Give me a sec," she said. "I'll pull some clothes on."

"Take your time. I trust you." He gave her a smile that was hard to read.

She wanted to jump out of the chair, kiss him, give him a squeeze, but he didn't look like he was in a squeezable mood.

"Thanks Frank," she said.

He waved, just a small flick of the wrist.

Clearly, she'd fucked things up.

The lock on the front door had clicked before she

redialed Fulin. "What's next?" she asked.

"They didn't believe me when I told them I didn't have sex with her. I told them I'd take a lie detector test."

"Who are 'they?'"

"Your ex-boyfriend and his dick of a partner. Joey Tufts told them I was obsessed with her. Her mother must've said something, too."

Lennox told him she'd go over to the Bauers' and talk to Rose.

She showered, did her dishes, and made the bed. Before she left the house, she sent Frank a text. Told him what a lovely time she'd had last night and how generally she was delightful company in the morning.

On the truth-o-meter, *delightful company in the morning* pegged deep on the whopper side of the scale. She went on to say that this was the first time she brought the phone to the table ever. Let's call that a white lie. She finished with the hope that he could look past this morning.

Then she headed over to Rose Bauer's residence. She stood on the Bauer stoop in the rain until Rose answered the doorbell. The old lady wore pink workout pants and a hoodie, the same design as the lavender set she wore the day Lennox met her. Above the round body was a face that had read the morning's headlines.

"I see you brought me the paper," she said. "Case I'd missed it." Deep lines ran down either side of her nose. Her mouth looked like it had never known a lick of joy.

Lennox was a cretin, bothering this nice lady when she should be sending her casseroles and cards with pictures of forests and words of comfort. "I'm so sorry. I can't tell you how sorry I am."

The old lady made no move to let her in out of the rain.

"I'm not trying to make trouble," Lennox continued.

"The last time you were here, in Matilda's room, what were you doing if not making trouble?" Rose said.

"Please let me talk to you for a minute. I promise I'll go when you tell me to. I just want you to know Fulin's a decent guy and he's getting blamed for Matilda's death."

"Fulin didn't kill Matilda," Rose said. "And I'll tell you another thing. There's some people wouldn't stand outside and ring my doorbell, they'd just break in."

"I don't understand," Lennox said.

She watched as the old lady made up her mind to unlock the storm door.

"Joey'd climb up the dogwood in the back yard, step over the roof like a cat, then down through Matilda's window. He was nine years old when they started up."

"I don't know what you mean by started up," Lennox said.

Rose's face curled with disgust. "What do you think I mean?"

"At *nine*?"

Joey was nine, making Matilda twelve years old, maybe not too young to do the kinds of experimenting Rose and her husband, Donald, had suspected them of. Rose and Donald had tried to discipline their daughter. Had exhausted themselves and broke their hearts trying. Donald had died early worrying about that girl. And it only got worse when he was gone and Matilda was well into her teens. Older boys with strange piercings. They mumbled and smoked in her house even when Rose told them not to.

Rose's face sagged as she continued with Matilda's history. "She seemed to turn a corner," Rose said. "She let her hair grow back to its natural color." But then Matilda started up with older men, got herself expelled, did Lennox know that? She had gotten caught with the principal of her school. He'd been fired, and she'd been expelled.

Making Hobby Glover not the only school principal Matilda had messed with.

As Rose talked, Lennox looked at the framed photos on Rose's mantle, all the pictures of Matilda, from childhood into her teens. Matilda was a pretty girl: big eyes, straight nose, a little pointed on the tip, high cheekbones, and a wide mouth. A photograph when she was four, with white-blonde braids. A pixie cut and a missing front tooth at six; black hair at thirteen. Blonde hair and careful eye makeup at fifteen. Fifteen going on twenty-five.

"How did Joey react to these other guys?" Lennox said.

"Matilda never stopped with him. I got so I could hear their muffled sounds in the middle of the night. Sometimes I'd go to wake her up and he was still in her bed. If I nailed the window into the sill, he'd take a hammer claw and pull the nails out. Both of them were incorrigible."

"Let me get this straight," Lennox said. "All these guys swarming around Matilda, and Joey never got jealous?"

"I never said that, but somehow Matilda always got around him."

"Rose, who do you think killed your daughter?"

Her face was filled with hate. "Joey killed her. Maybe they thought they were having a wild time, but he did it."

"He has a good alibi," Lennox said.

Rose snorted. Then she closed her eyes and sucked in her breath. "Mattie was here the whole time. When I was at church and after I got home. Had supper and went to bed. All Monday, too. Hanging there."

Tears ran down her cheeks, but she stiffened when

Lennox tried to hug her. She fished a tissue from the pocket of her hoodie and dabbed her face.

"I loved my daughter," she said, making motions of showing Lennox out. The "but—" hung in the air. Lennox waited for Rose to complete the thought. When she didn't, Lennox said, "You loved your daughter—"

"But I wish I still had Donald," Rose said.

CHAPTER 17

On the drive home from Rose's, Lennox kept picturing the old lady alone in that house, left with the memory of her dead daughter. "The first half of our life is ruined by our parents," some famous person wrote. "The second half by our children." Lennox wondered how disappointed her own mother was with her disgraced ex-cop of a daughter. All that happy family stuff was just a myth. She needed a drink. She called Fulin and told him to meet her at the Shanty and bring any research he'd dug up on the two suspects.

An old dude in a Gore-Tex parka sat at the far end of the bar reading the newspaper by the weak afternoon light of the Shanty's only window. The place smelled less like fried fish and more like spilled beer. Leprechauns, shamrocks and green garland for Saint Pat's festooned the supporting beams. Rows of Jameson and Bushmills whiskey stood lined up behind the bar, ready to be poured. In March at the Shanty, everyone was Irish.

Katy the cocktailer shoveled ice into bins behind the bar. Lennox waited for her to finish before ordering her

Blarney on the rocks.

"You're here early," Katy said. "Everything okay?"

"Sort of," Lennox said.

Katy leaned over the bar and said in a low voice, "Some of the guys have been talking. It's not true about Fulin, right? Because he wouldn't do anything like that?" Like stringing up a girl and pulling her knickers down. And watching her slowly choke to death.

"No, he wouldn't, Katy," Lennox said. She was absolutely firm about that. And she knew Katy would take Lennox's word as hard fact. If any whispers about Fulin arose, Katie would quash them because her detective buddy said so.

Lennox walked past the bar to a corner table. She booted her laptop and started working on Matilda's database. One of these people in Matilda's database had learned the truth about Matilda and gone after her. Say it wasn't Hobby Glover. Then why the autoeroticism bullshit, and why the little girl get-up? According to Sarge, the only signs of struggle appeared around her neck area, her legs below the knee, and under her fingernails. Indicating she'd started to choke and clawed at the ligature to loosen it. Maybe the killer wasn't trying to put a stop to blackmail.

Maybe Joey and Matilda were playing rough, and then all her betrayals and her duplicity suddenly enraged him. He grabbed her by the legs and yanked down, so that she was sure to choke and die. The same scenario worked for Debbie, if they were lovers. But that was not yet proven.

Maybe it was something different. Maybe Debbie discovered that Matilda had broken into her files and was scamming her clients.

She glanced up and saw Fulin headed towards her dressed in going-to-the-attorney clothes, slacks and an oxford shirt. He looked like he'd just been delivered some more bad news. Kline wouldn't have turned him down as a client?

"How's it going?" she said. By which she meant, *what's wrong?* She dreaded what he might tell her.

"I just got done with Kline and I was called in for a police line-up," he said.

It was all she could do to keep from hyperventilating. Katy came to the table and took Fulin's drink order. Gave him a big warm smile. He was so in his head, Katy could've disrobed and he wouldn't have noticed.

"A line-up means a witness," Lennox said. "Do you know who it is?"

Of course not.

"And Tommy put it together," she said.

"It was all about the hair," he said. "An old guy with a stringy ponytail, a fat dude that could pass for the Big Lebowski, a black man with dreads, they even had a woman with long red hair. No other Asian guys, no guy that was even as tall as me."

"So it's about the black braid," she said. Her mind was freaking racing. They were running out of time before Tommy built enough of a case to arrest Fulin.

"We've got three good suspects," she said. "Any one of them could have done it. We're not that far from solving this."

Fulin nodded, but he knew the score. They had three suspects with possible motives and means, but nothing definitive.

Katy brought him his drink.

"How did it go with Kline?" Lennox said.

"I don't know." Fulin shrugged. "I told him about the

blackmail. I told him I fudged the records, how I hired you to help me find Matilda. He told me to call him when I'm arrested."

Like that was a given.

He straightened in his chair. "I found some interesting stuff on Emily Cross," he said.

Fulin. Most guys, no matter how tough they thought they were, would have been paralyzed or blind drunk after a day like Fulin had had. But he had sucked it up and went back to work. The guy had guts.

Fulin pulled out his research. Emily Cross lived in an apartment on southeast Yamhill. She had two sisters, both married. Emily was the middle child. She'd worked for Joan Strake for the last year and a half. And here was the good part: she was a convicted felon. Yup. She and Matilda Bauer had served time at the Copper River Women's Penitentiary. Their sentences overlapped.

"You're shitting me," Lennox said.

"Emily went down for bank robbery," he said. Turned out she drove the getaway car. She was seventeen at the time, but the judge came down on her hard. She got the job at Geitner as part of an outreach program some liberals cooked up to rehabilitate female inmates. First Emily gets a job working for Joan Strake, then when Matilda gets out, she also gets a job working for the same woman. It was unusual.

Fulin agreed.

"Was Matilda in the same outreach program?"

"She dropped out."

"So I need another interview with Emily," she said. There was a long moment of silence. Lennox picked up her drink, and so did Fulin. She'd bet the pot they were both thinking the same thing: when was he going to be arrested?

CHAPTER 18

Bad news. If you can see it coming, you brace yourself; you weigh the outcome. But there's always that niggling voice, that voice of hope whispering, "Maybe it's good news." Whether you can admit it or not, that little whisper is a potent thing. Lennox could see that bit of hope on Fulin's face as she got off the phone with Sarge.

She had to tell him. He'd been ID'd in the police line-up. Fulin's eyes turned scared. They skittered from her face to the walls of her office, then down the hall. She didn't know if he was looking for something to do or somewhere to hide. She wanted to offer him a glass of water, or a plan.

"Finish your search on Joan Strake," she said, with as much optimism as she could muster. "And while you're at it, call Joan's receptionist, see if you can't charm her into setting up an interview. Tell her all we need is fifteen minutes. I'm going to have a conversation with Emily Cross. We'll work double-time until we find the murderer."

Fulin sat with his back to her, his spine erect, his long black braid hanging over the chair back. Fulin was typing something into a search engine when she left the house.

• • •

The smell of tobacco mixed with the smell of rain and the wet boxwoods lining the walks at Geitner Graphics. Lennox stood with her back against the brick facade of the building and fake smoked. Cars splashed past the campus as they hit the puddles on the parkway. Finally, Emily came outside for a butt break.

"Emily," she said.

Emily was dressed in a frumpy knit skirt that hugged her hips and thighs. She gave Lennox a puzzled smile and said hi. "I'm sorry, I've forgotten your name."

"Lennox. Remember, we talked about Matilda a little bit? I saw you at her funeral."

Emily nodded. She pulled her wine-colored cardigan closer to her body and shivered. Her pale cheeks were turning pink in the cold. "It was such a shock," she said. She pulled her cigarettes out of her sweater pocket. Her nails were painted in wine and white stripes. Her hands trembled as she lit up.

Lennox crushed her half-smoked cigarette in the planter and reached into her bag for her license. "I have a few questions to ask you about Matilda."

Emily scanned the license. "Oh," she said in a little voice, like she knew all along no one would be friendly to her without an agenda.

"I'm sorry," Lennox said.

Emily lit her cigarette. Her hands shook. "What did you want to ask me?" she said.

"Did you get Joan to hire Matilda?"

Emily told her she did.

"You met Matilda when you were at Copper River?"

"We were friends," Emily said. "We used to have lunch together every day. I told her about the retraining program that reduces your sentence."

"I did some searching on your background," Lennox said. "I got to tell you, you just don't look like a bank robber."

"What does a bank robber look like?" Emily said.

"No offense," Lennox said. "Kind of stupid."

Emily smiled that sweet, guileless smile she had. "I was stupid. I was in love."

And she was just out of high school when she drove the getaway car, poor kid.

"We all make mistakes at that age," Lennox said. "It was shitty luck you got caught."

Emily grinned then stubbed out her cigarette in the planter. "You robbed a bank when you were a kid?"

Well, no.

"I gotta get back to work," she said.

"One more question," Lennox said. "Why didn't Joan fire Matilda? She called in sick all the time."

"I don't know," Emily said. "You'd have to ask Joan that one." She had that complicated expression Lennox had noticed the first time she met Emily.

"One more," Lennox said. And she knew she was pushing her luck, asking all this personal stuff. Emily could've told her to fuck off from the get-go. "Were you still friends with Matilda after she got out of Copper River?"

Emily looked down at her shoes. "Once she got out, she had other friends," she said. She pulled her sweater closer to her body. "Gotta go."

The rain stopped as Lennox pulled from the parking lot back into traffic, but the cloud cover barely cleared the high-rises downtown. It had been over a week since she had seen the mountains or the sky. She turned on defrost and maneuvered through traffic. She drove into her driveway just as a navy Crown Vic pulled in behind her. A squad car, its blue and reds flashing, pulled up to the curb.

Two uniforms emerged from the squad car, their weapons drawn and against their thighs. They walked up the driveway until they were even with the Crown Vic. That's when Tommy got out of the car. Like he needed firepower to arrest Fulin. Like he hadn't known Fulin for the last ten years, knew that he'd never resist the law. She hated Tommy more in this moment than she'd ever hated him. And that was saying a lot.

"Get back in your vehicle, Cooper," Tommy said.

"Or what?" she said. "You're going to shoot me?"

"Make her get back in her truck," he said to the dark-haired uniform. "If she resists, cuff her."

Lennox climbed back into her Bronco.

She rolled down her window and watched as Tommy Pavlik pulled his gun out and held it against his chest, the barrel pointed up. He pounded on her front door and yelled, "Open the door, it's the police."

One second later, he motioned to the uniforms to kick the door down. Pavlik knew better than to try this move himself. Her door was steel enforced. She'd investigated enough break-ins to know what hollow core doors bought you.

Fulin answered the door before anyone had to injure themselves. He was dressed all in black, his hair neatly braided, his posture regal. She watched Fulin as Tommy read him his rights off a laminated card that he stuffed back into his seedy-looking sports jacket. Fulin kept his face from betraying any emotion. He straightened his arms in front of him for Tommy to cuff. Tommy led him to the squad car and placed his hand on top of Fulin's head to guide him inside. Lennox tipped her chin up and made a brave face in case Fulin looked her way. He kept his head facing forward.

Old lady Kurtz from across the street twitched her drapes closed as the police drove away.

CHAPTER 19

Lennox and Frank were the last two to join the Friday night poker game. You could have cut the gloom with a butter knife. Fulin's chair was empty next to Jerry. The green felt in front of Fulin's seat still showed the stain where Jerry had spilled his scotch the time he hit four of a kind. The room smelled of whiskey, dirty carpet, and Ham's Berkeley warm-up jacket.

Ham hadn't even broken the seal on the cards. The chips were still in the case. Could they even play, knowing that Fulin was stuck in jail?

"The line-up was ridiculous," Sarge said. "It was all about the hair."

"What we figured," Lennox said.

"Did he tell you they had a woman in the line-up?" Sarge said.

"Fucking Tommy," Fish said. He raked his fingers though his too-thick hair.

"Can Catholics say fucking?" Ham said.

"You think Jesus doesn't know what a fuckhead

Tommy is?" Fish said.

Sarge sucked the beer off his mustache. "Maybe if Lennox hadn't broken his nose?"

"It's not about me!" Lennox said.

"Let's face it," Ham said. "He hates all of us."

"He doesn't have a lot on Fulin," Lennox said. "A black wig and some fudged reports."

"Are you kidding?" Fish said. "You don't think falsifying reports is a big deal? Plus he was brought in for fighting over her with the chick's boyfriend. Those photos."

"I haven't seen the forensics," Lennox said. "But far as I know, there's no proof Fulin was ever in that room."

"I'll get us some beers." Frank said. Frank. She'd forgotten him for a minute. He got up from the table, closing the door behind him.

"When is Kline getting the discovery?" Jerry said. Jerry was looking rough. His face had more creases than his suit.

"There are some things to nail down yet," Lennox said.

"Like what?" Jerry said. His voice went all edgy and suspicious.

"Fulin's talked to Kline," Lennox said. "But he hadn't been charged with anything at the time. Strictly speaking, Kline hasn't been hired yet."

"Why the fuck not?" Jerry said. The edge on his voice had grown a roll of razor wire over it. "What were you doing all day?"

"Kline was in court," Lennox said. "I've got an appointment with him tomorrow. Why are you jumping my shit?"

Frank came back in the room. "Guys, I can hear you outside."

Ham had yet to distribute chips. Frank settled in his

chair. Lennox thanked him for the beer. Tried to get a read on him. What she got was a carefully neutral face. He was trying to stay out of it. Wise man.

"You've been working on the Bauer case a week," Sarge said in this hopeful little voice. Like a math teacher wishing you'd done your homework. "You have some good theories on who else could've done it?"

Lennox lined out her suspects. Sarge, Jerry, and Fish whipped out their little notebooks, taking notes like crazy.

Ham sighed. "Who wants to buy some chips?"

Lennox threw in fifty bucks. The first one to throw in; the first one to keep on keeping on. When she was in trouble, it was the poker that kept her going. Shoulder to shoulder with the men who talked trash, faked each other out, and played the possibilities. So Fulin couldn't play this time. She had to believe that he would feel better that they were together. That they weren't just playing—they were holding him in their circle.

They all threw in money. The crazy sound of chips stacking in piles. The lovely little wooden chips that made that smacking sound. It distracted her for a minute or two.

"What about that Emily chick you were talking about?" Fish said.

Sarge nodded and made a note in his notebook. The light from the fake Tiffany poker lamp bounced reflections off his bald head.

"Emily was Matilda's coworker," Lennox said. "The only reason she'd have to kill Matilda was her lousy attendance record."

"She knew Matilda in the joint," Sarge said.

"There you go," Jerry said.

She said. "Haven't I brought in the right guy hundreds

of times?"

"They're just trying to help," Frank said to Lennox.

"No offense," Fish said. "But you're not law enforcement."

It got very quiet.

Ham broke the silence peeling the strip of cellophane off a new deck of cards. "Five-card stud," he said. He dealt everyone a hole card followed by a face-up card.

"Fish with king-high," Ham said.

Fish threw in two red chips. Sarge, Frank, and Lennox checked. Their chips clacked against each other.

"Speak up," Lennox said. "Is my judgment being questioned?"

"It's not like that," Jerry said. "Fold. But why hasn't Kline committed one way or the other? Is it the money?"

Lennox shrugged. "I don't know what his problem is," she said. "I'll find out tomorrow."

Ham threw in two chips and dealt the next round of cards. Frank got zip; Lennox landed her third nine. Glory, glory. Fish drew a two of hearts.

"Possible flush," Ham said, mucho glum.

Sarge drew an ace of clubs.

"Possible straight," Ham said.

Sarge's gray mustache drooped over his unhappy mouth. "Our boy's in jail," he said. He threw in his chips.

That was it. Fulin was their boy and therefore different from all the clients she had defended in the past. "You all are wondering if I'm up to it," she said.

A chorus of nos. A "No" even coming from Frank. She wished he'd stay the hell out of it.

"What about Rose?" Fish said. "She has the same motive as Joey. Think about it. Years of trouble, behavior

119

that galled the old lady to the bone. She practically blames Matilda for her husband's death. She walks up the stairs with a stack of folded laundry, sees Matilda in that get-up putting on a sex act. Loses it. Kicks the stool out and goes back downstairs. Drives to the church for the afternoon service."

"Could a mother do that?" Frank said. Good for Frank.

A chorus of "Shit, yeah!"

Male cops.

"Think of the ick factor," Lennox said. "No mother in the world."

"How do you know?" Fish said. "You're not a mother."

"Neither are you," she said.

"All I'm saying is the chick didn't invent kinky sex. Most vice cases you find the acorn didn't fall far from the tree," Fish said.

"Trust me," Lennox said. "That little acorn not only fell far from the tree, it rolled itself into an entirely different neighborhood."

The room turned quiet. Ham burped. Then turned over his card and checked. "It's blackmail," he said. "Anytime you have blackmail on the table, that's where you'll find the murderer."

That seemed to reanimate the guys. Sarge made a note in his notebook.

"Ham's got a point," Jerry said. "How many people did the woman have her hooks into?"

Sarge waited expectantly, pen poised. Five sets of eyes drilled into her. This whole night was a drill. She was sitting on three nines, only the pair showing; she ought to be in heaven. She pulled from her beer. Wiped the corners of her mouth with her cocktail napkin. Gave herself a few seconds to think. She felt defensive. She knew that. Was it justified?

She decided to answer Jerry's question.

"Three in town here. More if you count the out-of-towners."

"Someone could've hired the hit," Ham said.

Lennox shook her head. "If someone hired a professional hit, they sure as hell wouldn't have set it up that way."

"Point," Jerry said.

Ham sat with his big hand covering the deck. The game had halted halfway.

"I've got a pair of nines here," Lennox said. "Are we going to play or what?"

She threw in three chips.

Ham dealt another round of cards face-up. She drew an eight of clubs. Sarge paired his ace and led the next round of betting. Lennox raised.

Sarge reraised. Just her and Sarge left for the last card, and a small mountain of chips on the table. Showtime.

Two pair for Sarge. Lennox scooped the pot with her three nines.

Jerry gave her less than a minute to enjoy her win before he peppered her with more questions.

The rest of the night was more of the same. All their "brainstorming" and "help" left her crabbier than hell. Even the $200 she'd taken off them didn't help.

It had stopped raining when Lennox and Frank stepped outside the Shanty for the walk back to her house. They crossed Forty-seventh, Frank taking her hand.

"You played a good game tonight," he said.

A fat plop of water fell on her head from the branches overhead. She shivered. Frank dropped her hand and wrapped his arm around her back.

"All these years," she said. "My years in vice. Then homicide. Hundreds of investigations. Did you know that? Hundreds."

Frank squeezed her closer to him.

She shook off his arm. "Listen to me."

"I am," he said.

"They don't trust me. Their boy Fulin, and they don't think I'm up to the job."

"Slow down," Frank said. "The guys are just trying to help."

"Yeah, well they've never tried to help on my other murder investigations."

She and Frank walked the next three blocks in silence. Another bloated raindrop fell on her cheek. She wiped it away with the back of her hand.

Frank said, "Have you ever thought, maybe Fulin...?"

"There is no fucking way," she said. "You don't know him. You don't know any of us."

A mean thing to say. She knew it the millisecond it came out of her mouth, but she didn't take it back.

They halted on the sidewalk outside her house. Her porch light threw a yellow halo next to her door.

He cleared his throat. She took a long look at him. How damned cute he was with his eyes black in the low light, that divot in his chin. He was a nice man.

"Are you going to ask me in?" he said.

And she knew she should. She should put this whole investigation away from her. Roll around in the sack with the lovely, good man Frank was.

She wrapped her arms around herself. What was wrong with her? She said, "I'd be no kind of company tonight."

CHAPTER 20

If your problem happened to be of a criminal nature, Bowersox, Kline & Hansen were the go-to law firm. August Kline was the youngest and smartest of the partners, and though he came off as a stick-up-the-ass, he was a good guy to work for. Ever since the Pike case, Lennox had been his sleuth of choice.

Lennox rode the two elevators up to the aerie Kline called an office. The air smelled clean and sharp like it was oxygenated. And sky. Sky, wherever you looked. Only right now the sky was the color of week-old snow and streaked with heavy clouds. Beneath her, the southeastern part of the city stretched across the valley floor and climbed Mount Tabor, a lava cone that loomed over the Hawthorne district.

Sloane, the friendlier of Kline's two admins, offered Lennox a cup of coffee and ushered her into Kline's office.

August Kline leaned back in his chair, his short legs stretched forward, his feet propped on the half-acre he called a desk. His face lit up when he saw Lennox. He motioned her to a chair.

"Who do you have for me?" Kline said.

"Fulin Chen."

Kline swung his legs down. "I was afraid of that."

"What do you mean?"

"I met him. He's a schmuck. And he's been in the media non-stop," he said. "No."

"Why are you calling him a schmuck? He's innocent."

Kline looked at her skeptically.

"I know him," Lennox said. "He's been a close friend for over ten years."

"For Chrissake," he said. "Lennox, he was having cyber sex with his parolee. Or does Channel 4 have it wrong?"

"Didn't he explain that to you? He would never take advantage of a client. He'd never kill anyone. The murder victim set him up."

"The case is already on the national networks." Kline shook his head. "I can talk to Bowersox, but I'll tell you right now, he's not going to like it. He's against the firm working on any sex crimes."

"Come on, Gus," she said. "The only thing my guy did wrong was not turning in the victim the minute he found out about her. And Tommy Pavlik's investigating. You know how he is. Makes up his mind before the crime scene is even done processing."

Kline groaned. "On top of the guy getting national attention, we've got Tommy Pavlik. This is one steaming pile you've brought me."

Lennox felt her ears get hot. Kline knew she had a long, ugly history with Tommy. She didn't know whether she was mad or embarrassed. "At least I won't have to work with the scraps left behind from a thorough investigation," she said.

"You're sure Chen's innocent?"

"One hundred percent."

"Those are the worst," he said.

"Why?"

"When we know the client is guilty, we can go forward. What is it about the client that led him to the crime. Troubled childhood, mental problems, etc. You know how it works. It's the innocent client who's the mess."

"The Pike murder," Lennox said.

"That's what I mean. Our client was a disaster, and they're all like that one way or another. They do stupid things because they know they're innocent."

"Fulin's not like that," she said. "Let me tell you how it went down."

Sloane brought Kline and Lennox two more cups of coffee and an extra sugar packet for Lennox. Lennox was still recounting the sequence of events as the sky grew darker, and it began to rain again. She watched the vertical streaks over Mount Tabor.

Kline sipped his coffee and made notes from time to time.

"I don't know," he said.

"It was a setup from the beginning," she said. "He should've turned her in immediately, but he knew he'd lose his job."

When she finished, he said, "You've got two witnesses: Joey Tufts saying Fulin beat him up over the victim, and a neighbor saying she saw Fulin go to the back of the house within an hour of the murder. Fulin's admission that he had cyber sex with the victim. He hires you before he's charged with anything."

"You know how unreliable witnesses are," Lennox said.

"And how convincing," Kline said. He tore the sheet of paper he was making notes on and balled it up.

It occurred to her that Kline might actually refuse the case.

"The witness identified him from the back," she said. She was talking faster now, and could hear the edge in her voice. "Fulin's got a three-foot-long black braid. Anybody could have worn a wig."

"Tell me the witness is not an old lady," he said. "If I put her on the stand and question her judgment, she cries, and the jury hates me."

"I've got a head start. Five suspects: Joey Tufts, Hobby Glover, Debbie Paulson, Joan Strake, and Emily Cross, and Fulin was arrested yesterday. And you're telling me the case is too hard for you?"

"Chen's a cop," Kline said. "How is he even going to pay for both of us?"

"What is it, Gus?" she said. "Is it the money, the notoriety, or the fact you don't think you can win?"

Kline ran his fingers through his short, curly hair. "You know the statistics for not-guilty judgments. And how many of those people swear they're innocent? How many of those people are truly innocent? We have no way of knowing. They end up in prison for life or given the death sentence because we couldn't cast a reasonable doubt in the heads of the jurors. That's why I hate these cases."

Lennox folded her arms. She wasn't leaving until he agreed to take on the case. He steepled his fingers, and gazed over her shoulder at his stunning view. A few seconds went by. His gaze turned to her face, and then back to the view. You'd have to know how painful it was for Kline to just sit there, staring out the window, a guy who charged for his services by the minute. Money wasted. Lennox would give him another thirty seconds tops before he caved.

"Okay," he said. "I'll defend him, but you're going to build our case."

CHAPTER 21

She drove back through the rain to her office. Fulin's file on Joan Strake lay next to her keyboard. He must've been working on it when Pavlik came to arrest him. Not only had he printed the search pages and highlighted the pertinent information, he had used a couple of search engines Lennox had never heard of. The guy was a natural PI. It killed her thinking he was in jail.

She paged through the report. Turned out Joan Strake had been married once to a dude fifteen years her junior. No kids. They divorced three years ago and she was still paying spousal at the rate of four thousand per month. The hubby took half her assets and an additional fifteen thousand for retraining. In addition, she cashed him out of her 401Ks and paid the penalties. Which left her in a way-low cash position, a condo with a lofty mortgage, and two years of car payments left on her Jag. She still had some money left in those 401Ks, but not enough to retire in the next decade unless she was willing to relocate to Nebraska.

Fulin had combed through Joan's phone logs and

emails. She talked or wrote to her sister in Phoenix, an old college friend in Cleveland, and Matilda Bauer.

Bingo.

Matilda didn't show up in her emails, but off hours Joan had logged a significant time on the telephone with Matilda. It was noteworthy that neither Joan nor Matilda had many friends.

Fulin had traced a number of credit card slips to a spendy restaurant in The Pearl called The Blue Note. That was as far as he'd gotten before he was arrested.

* * *

Lennox woke up when she heard the doorbell. A persistent ring. She found herself face down on top of Joan Strake's file, a wet smear where she had drooled on the report.

Frank. She forgot how much she liked that square chin of his. And the little cleft. How thick and dark his hair was. How could she forget they had a dinner date?

He looked relieved to see her.

"I'm sorry," she said. "I fell asleep at my desk. I've been working really long hours."

"We could stay in if you want. Order takeout," he said.

It was such a relief not to go out. They ordered Mu-shu from the neighborhood Chinese joint. Frank uncorked a bottle of red while Lennox rummaged through her junk drawer for candles to make it seem more like a date. Frank poured them each a glass of wine.

They toasted to each other's health.

"How was your day?" he said.

"I spent the better part of the morning trying to convince the attorney to take the case. I guess it wore me out worse than I thought."

"Too big of a risk?" Frank said.

"It's complicated," she said.

"Of course it is."

She couldn't hear any irony in his voice, or pick up irony in his eyes, but she wasn't sure. She knew his body better than she knew his head. And she didn't want to ask him what he meant, in case what he meant would ruin the evening.

"How was your day?" she said.

Before he could answer, she pressed her lips against his and kissed him for a nice long time. She tasted the cabernet they'd just sipped from, and felt the warmth of his body, the overall sturdiness of him.

Frank had to put his clothes back on to pay the delivery guy when their food came.

CHAPTER 22

The very last person Lennox expected to see on her porch at seven in the morning was August Kline. He held a cardboard tray of Starbucks in one hand and a bulging briefcase in the other. This was a guy who never crossed the Willamette River unless he had tickets to a Blazer game, a guy who had minions upon minions to fetch his coffee, answer his mail, and courier his papers.

Outside it was still dark and foggy as hell. Lennox was in her jammies when she answered the door.

"The D.A. dropped off Fulin's discovery this morning," Kline said. "I needed a latte and figured I was halfway to your place, so I'd save you the trip."

First of all, the closest Starbucks to his office was a block away from his office and a good twenty-minute drive from her house, and that was if the gods of traffic were on his side. He was nervous about the case; that was why he couldn't wait to give her the discovery. His anxiety touched off hers. Kline followed her to her office in the back of the house and stacked the contents of his briefcase on her desk.

In the adjacent room, Frank was in the shower singing an old Kurt Cobain tune in a gravelly voice.

"Is this a bad time?" Kline said, getting for the first time that it might indeed be a bad time.

"No. How's Fulin holding up?" she said.

"He puts on a brave face."

While Kline sipped his coffee and watched the fog through her window, she sifted through the discovery. There were Matilda's parole records, and places where Fulin fudged her reports before her murder. There was Joey's statement: "The Chen guy was harassing her, man; he was obsessed." Screen-capture photos of Fulin masturbating in front of his computer. That way Tommy Pavlik made sure that Fulin Chen would never work in criminal justice again, whether he was acquitted or not. Lennox took a deep breath and turned the photos over. Kline leaned back in the office chair, watching the first sparrows of the morning fight over the seed husks in her feeder.

Lennox returned to the stack. She noted Sally Egan, the witness who'd ID'd Fulin entering the Bauer house at the approximate time of Matilda's murder. A set of Joey's fingerprints on the sill. Lennox read Joey's statement that he had climbed through the window to visit Matilda earlier in the week. Rose reluctantly confirmed his story. Other fingerprints belonging to Matilda were found on the closet doors and mirror frame, Rose's prints on the banister. The desk and file cabinets were wiped clean of prints.

"No sign that Fulin was at the murder scene," she said.

"Keep going," was Kline's grumpy reply.

An inventory was made of the contents of Matilda's room including the contents of her file cabinets and desk drawers.

"Where is her computer?" Lennox said.

"They didn't find one."

Lennox pulled out her photos of Matilda hanging from the ceiling. The dolls and stuffed bears arranged at the base of a full-length mirror behind her body. The way she was positioned to face the desk.

The stairs creaked with Frank's footsteps.

"If this was a lovers' tryst or a john, why wasn't she set up to face the bed?" she said. "She was positioned facing her desk. It looked staged for an internet customer. In which case, where's the computer?"

"The murderer must've taken it with him," Kline said.

"What do we have here?" she said. The identification of five long hairs found in Matilda's bedroom. Tommy's hair expert identified the hairs as human, consistent with Asian hair.

"Fulin," Kline said.

"But there's nothing in the report to indicate if they had the entire shaft of hair, and if they don't they can't get a blood type or a DNA sample."

That was the last report in the file.

"You're kidding me, this is all they have for discovery?" she said. "Who else did they look at for the crime?"

"Fulin was the obvious suspect."

"No, he wasn't," she said. "The victim had been making a living fleecing men since she was a teenager. Her own mother said as much."

Kline nodded. "We can plead down. Go for reckless endangerment."

"Chen's not going to do that," she said. "He's innocent. He was home the day of the murder watching TV and nursing a bruised jaw."

Kline pinched the bridge of his nose, his gaze unfocussed. "I wish he had an alibi."

Frank came down the stairs and stood by her office door.

Geez, she'd forgotten about him.

Again.

"I'm off," he said, looking a little sheepish, but crisp and buttoned-down, like a proper professional person, which is hard to do wearing yesterday's clothes. Lennox introduced him to Kline.

Kline's ears turned pink. Lennox had no idea why Kline was turning pink. What did he expect, showing up at her door at seven in the morning? She excused herself and walked Frank to the door.

Frank brushed his lips against her neck. "Call me tonight?" he whispered. She told him she'd be working late, but yes, she'd call him.

When she returned, Kline's ears had returned to normal.

"This is just the kind of skim-job case Tommy Pavlik's famous for."

"It's light, I grant you, but Pavlik's not as bad as you make him out to be."

The voice of reason: Kline with that careful, watchful face. He knew Tommy had fluffed the evidence when he ran the Pike investigation, but Kline had said he'd seen worse from the Portland Police Bureau. Lennox wanted to argue with Kline, but it would be like arguing with the wall.

There was only one way to prove Tommy did sloppy police work, and that was to impeach the case Tommy built against Fulin.

"Next steps?" Kline said.

"The hair. It doesn't say whether they found a blood type or genetic marker that would tie them to Fulin. Am I on the approved list to bring the hair to our lab?" she said.

"Yeah, they're expecting you. When are you going to see the witness who ID'd Chen?"

"Today," she said.

There was a short silence between them before Kline cleared his throat. "Tell me about these suspects you have."

"The most likely at this juncture is a guy named Hobby Glover. Matilda met him on a virtual reality site engaged in off-color behavior." Lennox described the activity, and that Matilda had been blackmailing him. She told Kline about her interview, and how Hobby had known that Lennox wasn't the person behind the Tildy avatar.

"What about Joey Tufts?" Kline said.

"He's on the short list. Matilda's mother is convinced Joey murdered Matilda. His alibi isn't as great as he thinks it is. Then there's Debbie Paulson. She's an honest-to-God matchmaker and a supposedly good friend of Matilda's. Either they were lovers or business partners, or both. Emily Cross was Matilda's coworker. She knew Matilda from their prison days and helped Matilda get the job at Geitner Graphics. I have that connection, but I don't have a motive for her. I haven't reached the last person of interest, Joan Strake, Matilda's boss. I don't have anything on her yet, but why would she hire two ex-felons, and why would she tolerate Matilda's lousy attendance record?"

"Have you asked her?" Kline said.

"Not yet," she said. "But if I have to stalk her, I'll get some answers from her before our next meeting."

Kline pushed off from his chair and buttoned his coat. "Your bird feeders are empty," he said as he left the house.

• • •

Oliver Labs was where the detectives at Portland Police Bureau took all their work. It was a matter of budgets. Oliver Labs was okay in a broad picture sort of way, but if you were looking for genius forensics, Dave Hatch at HDS Labs was the go-to man. Lennox signed the chain of custody log and dropped the hair off with Dave.

On to the witness who'd ID'd Fulin. Her name was Sally Egan, and she worked full-time at Tri-Met, the local transit authority. Lennox worked at her desk until late afternoon, before making her way to Sally's house. At five thirty, Ms. Egan pulled into her driveway in a two-year-old Prius.

Sally Egan had lived across the street from Rose Bauer for the last eight years. She was fifty-four, five six, plump, her hair short and yellow-blonde. She swung her legs out from the car, stood, and stretched her back. She wore black trousers and a pale blue blouse underneath a black wool coat.

"A girl detective," she said when Lennox introduced herself. "What's that like?"

Big question, and one Lennox didn't want to get into with a witness. Lennox said something rote. Sally gave her a look, like she knew she was getting shined on.

"So, I told this all to the police," she said. "It was that Fulin guy. Definitely. A man like that you don't forget. He had black shiny hair down to here."

She told Lennox she didn't spend much time in the front of her house where she would see the Bauer's comings and goings, except sometimes in the evenings when she watched her shows. Every once in a while, Sally noticed Matilda leaving the house with a man. How many men? Mostly the same man. A young man, curly blond hair, over six foot, good-looking. Lennox fished Joey Tufts' mugshot from her bag.

"Did he look like this man?"

"Oh, dear," Sally said. Make that affirmative.

Who else? Another tall man, chunky. Bald. An older guy, shorter, lots of brown hair. Had Sally ever witnessed any domestic disturbances at the Bauer house? Sally shrugged. Nothing to call the police about. Had she witnessed the fight on the Bauer front lawn Friday, March 2nd? No, she had not gotten home until ten that night.

"Had you seen Fulin Chen before the day of the murder?"

"Maybe once before?" Sally said. "It was a while back. He drove up about the time I got home from work."

Sally didn't remember what make of car Fulin was driving.

"Tell me about the day of the murder," Lennox said.

"Sunday. The sun came out after breakfast," Sally said. "You remember? I went out to do a little weeding in the front beds. So around eleven, I looked up and saw him. Fulin. He was wearing a black leather jacket. He has this thick braid that reaches past his waist, you know? I thought to myself, 'It's a sin to give a man a head of hair like that when there's gals like us can't grow it past our ears.'"

"Did you see what he was driving?"

Sally shook her head.

"How tall was he?" Lennox said.

"Tall," Sally said. "Six feet."

Did Sally get a good look at his face? Profile, and then as he was entering the house, he looked over his shoulder, and caught Sally staring at him.

"How did he react when he saw you looking?" Lennox said.

"He smiled. He had nice teeth."

"So, like this?" Lennox gave Sally a big toothy grin.

"Just like that," Sally said.

Lennox tried to remember what Fulin's teeth even looked like. Come to think of it, he didn't laugh, really; he chuckled, his lips covering his teeth.

How hard would it be impersonate Fulin from across the street? Joey could've done it. Joan Strake or Debbie Paulson could've done it. And what about Fulin's race? Sally didn't mention it in her statement or in the interview with Lennox. Seventy-eight percent of all witnesses that come forward are crackpots or just plain mistaken.

CHAPTER 23

Secrets. The truth is we all want to get to the bottom of other people's secrets. It starts when you're a kid, and you know your parents are withholding. Matilda built a career on becoming men's dirty little secret. And look how that worked out. Lennox was all in favor of the truth shining from whatever web of half-truths or flat-out lies a person's constructed to hide behind. Lennox paged through the notes she had on Hobby Glover.

The secret she was most interested in untangling was Hobby Glover's virtual life. And the next step was to talk to his wife, Ann. She taught piano from their home, so Lennox was reasonably sure of catching her during school hours when Hobby was still at work. She drove west to suburbia, where the Glovers lived.

The Glover house was nestled in a sea of ranch houses, looking like everything else on the block. The Glovers kept their yard and bushes meticulous. A thick border of daffodils lined the left side of the driveway and the walk that led to the house. Heather, azaleas, and daphne bloomed in the front garden. The lawn was a deep emerald green from the winter rains.

Lennox heard the piano on her way up the driveway, the stutter of two lines of music played, then played again. The sour notes, the halting cadence. It was ten-fifteen, which meant the student probably would finish on the half hour. Lennox walked back to her Bronco and waited.

At 10:35, a shambling man in his late fifties exited the Glovers' front door and walked down the driveway. Lennox waited for the man to drive away before she rang the doorbell.

Ann Glover was a small, trim woman in her late forties, with light brown hair that had just started to silver. Her features were small, her lips thin. The one striking feature was her eyes, which were large and a luminous blue. "May I help you?" she said.

Looking into those blue eyes, Lennox felt a niggle of guilt, but she went ahead anyway. She showed Ann her PI license and asked for a few moments of Ann's time.

"What's this about?" Ann said. Looking alarmed, she blocked Lennox's entry.

"I'm investigating the Matilda Bauer murder," Lennox said.

Ann's enormous eyes grew even larger. "I don't know anything about the woman other than what I've read," she said.

"Please, may I come in?"

Ann reluctantly opened the door wider. The living room wasn't furnished with sofas, coffee tables and easy chairs. Instead, a baby grand piano dominated the room. An upright piano took up the wall opposite the picture window. Two wing backed chairs stood in front of the window along with a large rubber plant. Ann sank into one of the chairs and motioned with her hand for Lennox to take the other one.

"Can you tell me what you and your husband were doing on Sunday, March 5th?" Lennox said.

"That's right before we left for our trip to the coast," she said. "We planned to leave that day, but my husband had last-minute responsibilities at the school."

Lennox tried to keep the excitement out of her voice. "Was your husband working at the school Sunday morning?"

"Tell me what this is all about," Ann said.

If she answered Ann's question, the lady would most likely show her the door. And Lennox was this close to clinching Hobby Glover's role in Matilda's death.

"It's a very simple question," Lennox said. "Won't you just answer it?"

Ann's lips pressed together and she shook her head.

Lennox reached into her bag and withdrew one of Kline's business cards. She handed it to Ann. "If you're unwilling to answer my questions, we'll have to subpoena you and your husband." She waited for Ann to consider the fallout, and watched Ann's bravado crumble in less than a minute.

"He worked Sunday morning," Ann said. "Something about absenteeism. The administrative records not balancing, the secretary said. I don't remember. He didn't get home until lunch time."

Timing slotted alongside motive and means. Lennox would check whether the school secretary could verify Hobby's alibi, but she was still loving him for the crime.

"Does your husband play computer games?"

"Yes. But I don't understand what that has to do that

young woman's death."

"Do you know about Second Life?" Lennox said.

"No," Ann said. "Is that a computer game?"

The only question Lennox had left to ask her was about the $5000 plus Hobby had spent in blackmail in the last year. If Ann didn't know about Hobby's activity on Second Life, how likely was she to know about the blackmail? Hobby stood to lose his wife along with his career. Would Ann stand by him? Once you erode trust in a relationship, what's left to work with?

Ann's whole face sagged. "Did my husband know this Matilda Bauer?" she said.

"I'm not sure," Lennox said.

Secrets.

It wasn't up to Lennox to reveal one spouse's secrets to the other unless the information she would glean would help her investigation. Losing his career was motive enough for Hobby to want to kill Matilda.

By talking to Ann, Lennox had lit a slow fuse. Ann was sure to ask Hobby what was going on, so either he'd come to Lennox and answer her questions, or he'd come gunning for her.

When Lennox got home, there were two calls on her message phone. The first was from her lab. Nothing definite without the entire hair shaft, but her lab expert pegged the hair as Asian and belonging to a female. The second call was from Kline. Fulin would be released from jail in two days. Kline said he'd pick up Fulin; they needed to go over the case.

CHAPTER 24

The day started off with rotten news: a call back from the secretary at Cedar Hills High School. On the day of Matilda's murder, she had worked with Mr. Glover from nine until noon. It was still possible Ann Glover had erred or lied about when Hobby returned that day. It was a slim hope.

Lennox ended her afternoon across the street from Hill Construction. It was quitting time. She leaned against Joey Tufts' pickup and waited for him. When he saw her, he told her to get away from his truck, he didn't have to talk to her, he'd signed a piece of paper that protected witnesses from further stress caused by people such as herself.

"Forget the paper," she said. "We both want the same thing: to find Matilda's killer."

"Everyone knows who killed Mattie. The Chink."

"Chen was set up," she said.

"Bullshit! Remember, I saw your suspect list. I was on it."

"Are you sitting in jail?" she said. "No, because you've got a solid alibi. Let me buy you a coffee, pick your brain."

"I hate coffee."

"Beer. Whatever," she said. "Joey, I can show you my cases; I'm a hell of a detective. You can help me find Matilda's killer. You could tell me what she was really like, who her friends and enemies were, and who she was scared of. You knew her better than anyone."

She could almost hear him thinking how he hated cops, and if he respected her more, he'd hate her, too. He missed Matilda, and what if Lennox was right, and Mattie's killer was still out there, free?

"I don't have to tell you shit," he said.

"I didn't have to let you go free when you broke into my house and assaulted me," she said. She watched him think that over.

"Buy me a drink. Magoo's," he said. "You know it?"

"So you'll meet me there?" she said.

He grinned. Nodded.

Sure.

Lennox got to Magoo's first and ordered a beer from a very polite bartender who wore a Harley Davidson tee shirt stretched across his thirty-two percent fat index.

Joey no-showed. If she got paid for every time a witness blew her off she could buy Magoo's and give Mr. Polite a raise. But Joey—that guy was making her seriously question why she hadn't had him arrested for assault when she had the chance.

She drank up, tipped extravagantly. Next stop: Joey's house, in the heart of Felony Flats.

Joey had parked his rig in front of his house. He lived in a one-story decaying stucco job, surrounded by a cyclone fence. The grass was in need of a mow. Several paint cans leaned against the porch steps. The March frogs sang over the traffic noise on Foster as she locked her truck. The air felt cold and at the same time smelled of spring.

Two men sat smoking on the porch as she unlatched the gate and walked up to the house. A rangy, good-looking black man in his mid-forties smiled at her in the way that men do when they like what they see. The other man, skinny and pinched-looking, glanced at her once, then turned away. They anchored either end of a derelict sofa drinking beer.

When she got to the porch, she ignored them and banged on the front door.

"No need to go knocking, Mama, I'm right here," the handsome man said.

"I'm looking for Joey," she said.

"He's not here," said the skinny, rodent-faced one.

"Sure he is," she said. "There's his truck."

"You calling me a liar?" Rodent got threat into his voice.

"Forget about Joey. Have a beer with me," said Handsome.

"She's a cop, Tyrell," Rodent said.

"You're too cute to be a cop," Tyrell told Lennox.

Lennox banged harder on the front door. "Let me in Joey," she shouted.

No answer. Could this guy be more of an asshole?

"He doesn't want to talk to you," Tyrell said. "*I'll* talk to you. All night long, if that's what works for you."

Lennox turned the door handle. The door swung slowly in. "Tyrell, do I have your permission to enter?"

Tyrell. He was such an agreeable guy.

She pushed the door open straight into a dark living room. Joey sat in the glow of a huge flat screen, watching Hollywood gossip.

"I'm a protected witness," he said. "So get the hell out."

"Tyrell said I could come in."

"I'll kick his ass," Joey said.

"You can't get past the fact that a cop is probably going down for Mattie's murder. It must mean more to you than catching Mattie's real killer."

"Sure," Joey said. "Matilda would love it, her P.O. going to jail."

His attention drifted back to the television. She'd tried reasoning with the guy, she'd tried cutting him a break. He was like Joan Strake; the only thing left were threats.

"Tony Giordano," she said.

And watched him flinch. "Your P.O.?" she reminded him. "Great slow dancer. Lousy at cards. That face can't bluff, you know? You've probably noticed he's not been looking at you too kindly. Fulin's a buddy of his. Just wait 'til Tony hears *my* version, I bet I can have you back at the academy in less than a week."

Joey watched her, the television forgotten. She finally had his attention.

"Tell me about Matilda. How did she get that corporate job? She must've been good with computers."

"Naw. She learned it all on the job."

"So how did she get the job?" Lennox said. "Was her boss hot for her?"

He grinned. "Her boss is a woman."

"And?"

"Yeah. Maybe." He shrugged. "Everyone loved Mattie."

"Did you know Matilda was running a side business?" she said. "Making a whole lot of money swindling people on the internet?"

Joey let out a yip and started laughing. "Sure thing," he said. "You think I'm stupid, I don't know what my woman was up to. The answer is, I don't know the details, but I know."

"And you wouldn't be surprised if Matilda had had a lesbian relationship?"

Joey's face lit and was shadowed by the television's endless parade of commercials: manic images in primary colors for frozen dinners, tires, beer, and chain restaurants.

"She was wild," he said. "Some people call themselves that, they're just mental. Mattie could be anybody. She could do—anything. I never knew what I was going to get. Sometimes I'd want her to quit acting, be herself, goddamn it. I knew her better than anybody. We were just kids when we started up. We trusted each other."

"Who was Matilda afraid of?" she said. "Who were her friends other than you and Debbie?"

"Matilda didn't have friends," he said. "She had suckers."

He leaned back in his recliner and ratcheted up the volume on his remote. Lennox heard about all the shrimp she could eat! At $9.99!

Joey could've killed Matilda accidentally. Maybe they played the edge too close—and Matilda fell off to the other side? Maybe he told himself that Matilda playing sex games with other people was okay by him, until it wasn't okay.

That alibi Joey thought was so ironclad would be a cinch to crack.

CHAPTER 25

It was after eight when Lennox pulled into the driveway. Fulin's BMW was parked at the curb.

He was back.

She ran to the front door where he met her with the biggest grin. Even though she was stupid with happiness and relief, her detective radar kicked in. There are people with smiles so wide you can count their fillings and there are people who only smile with their lips. Fulin was definitely in the second camp.

He threw his arms wide, and they hugged a long time. It was better than heaven to have a friend to come home to.

"There's pizza left," he said.

"Naw," she said. "Let's go for a run."

He told her sure.

She climbed the stairs to her bedroom, stripped, and pulled on her workout clothes. Pulled her hair back in a ponytail and tied her running shoes. When she came downstairs, Fulin had pulled a fleece over his tee shirt.

They headed east from 52nd and Broadway, the street

lit by porch lights and streetlights, Fulin keeping easy pace with her.

"That witness who saw you at the Bauers' on Sunday morning said you smiled at her," Lennox said. "She said you had beautiful teeth."

"I do," he said.

"You smiled at her. You had beautiful teeth."

Fulin glanced over at her, puzzled.

"You don't show your teeth when you smile."

"It's a cultural thing," he said. A bead of sweat rolled down the side of his face.

"It's going to sink her testimony," Lennox said. She told him that her lab expert would testify that the hairs in evidence tying Fulin to the crime came from a female. "As in wig," Lennox said. She told him to turn left on 72nd.

They started the gradual climb up to the glacial ridge that crowned Rose City Park.

"I've got a chance at beating this," he said. "You're amazing."

It started to sprinkle.

"Aren't you getting winded?" Lennox said.

"I could run forever," he said.

"Have you found out anything more on Joan Strake?" she said.

"She had a bunch of credit card charges to a restaurant in The Pearl. The Blue Note?"

"Spendy," Lennox said.

"So I found a bartender who works there and knows her. She's a good tipper. He's seen her leave a couple times with young guys."

How young? Late twenties. And Joan was fifty-two. Fulin combed through her phone calls. No personal calls made to men.

"One night stands?"

"Looks like," Fulin said.

"It seems like her contacts should be a little messier than family and one friend. You know?"

"I thought so too. I'm still looking," he said.

"I'm so glad you're back," she said. "But can we turn around?"

"I'm hungry," she said in way of an explanation. In truth, she was hungry, thirsty, and tired to the bone.

* * *

The next morning, Lennox joined the rush hour crowd as she inched along the freeway, heading west. Forty-five minutes later, she pulled into the Geitner Graphics parking lot.

Lennox walked in with a crowd of damp and barely-on-time employees, and rode the elevator to Suite 310. Two admins sat at a pale green quartz counter: one was Emily Cross, the other a fresh-faced new girl. Twenty-three, Lennox would guess. Blonde, fit, size six, never been in trouble, never even contemplated trouble. The girl wore an engagement ring with the world's tiniest diamond. She looked happy.

Not Emily. She was scared to death. "Joan can't see you," she said in a low whisper of a voice.

"She'll either see me or she'll be slapped with a subpoena," Lennox said.

The new girl looked from Emily to Lennox. The phone rang, and the new girl answered it.

"I need this job," Emily said.

"There's nothing you've told me I couldn't have found

out by other means," Lennox said in a low voice. "I promise, I'll be careful."

Emily rang into Joan's office, then told Lennox to go on in.

Joan sat behind her long, narrow desk in a drapey ivory silk blouse. She wore a heavy gold bracelet around her wrist and chunky gold earrings in her ears, all of which must've cost a fortune.

"May I?" Lennox said, pulling out a chair facing the desk.

"You're getting to be quite the pest," Joan said. "I want to get something straight right now. This is our only interview."

"Usually admins are screened and hired by Human Resources," Lennox said. "But you went outside normal channels to hire Matilda yourself. Why is that?"

"You realize that I don't have to answer."

"That's true," Lennox said. "But I thought maybe you'd be interested in helping us find Matilda's murderer."

Joan leaned forward. "According to the news, the police have their murderer," she said in a soft voice.

"You haven't answered my question," Lennox said.

Lennox watched her decide whether to stonewall, or give Lennox a few crumbs.

"Our Human Resources did an outreach program with a women's prison," Joan said. "The prison trained the more promising inmates, and we hired a few women. They placed Emily Cross as my assistant, and she's worked beautifully, so I thought I'd try Matilda."

This much Lennox knew. "But Matilda never completed the skills program at the prison. According to her friends, she was hopeless with technology."

Joan shook her head. Her sleek hair swung in a perfect arc. "She seemed to make out all right," she said.

"Were you partners with Matilda in a side business?" Lennox said.

"I work sixty, sometimes seventy hours a week," Joan said. "I have no side business."

"Were you lovers?"

A flush traveled up the neckline of Joan's blouse. "Excuse me?" You could've flash-frozen meat with that voice.

"Matilda had poor office skills, and had used up all her personal days for the year calling in sick. What other reason would you keep her around?"

Joan picked up her phone and punched numbers. "I need security pronto. Suite 310."

"Consider yourself a witness for the defense," Lennox said. "A hostile witness. You're going to have to answer these questions now or in a courtroom."

"I don't have time to micromanage my staff," Joan said. "The work gets done. That's all I care about."

"Emily was doing Matilda's work."

Joan smiled without a gram of mirth. "Emily's been complaining, has she?"

"I don't have to be a detective to know how offices work," Lennox said. "Somebody has to pick up the slack."

Joan's phone lit up. A moment later she told Lennox that security would like to accompany her to her vehicle.

CHAPTER 26

It was eight in the morning and raining when Fulin walked through the front door of the Bijou Cafe. The Bijou was a hip, funky little place smack in the middle of Old Town, a place where the young drunks drink and drug side by side with the homeless. Old Town was both beautiful and derelict, with its homeless camped alongside the historic fountains and cast iron facades.

The cafe was full when Fulin showed up, ten minutes late. Lennox put her coffee cup down and waved him over. He was scowling as he flung himself in a chair. "I saw my folks this morning," he said.

"How do you even do that before you've had your coffee?" she said.

"Ma won't talk to me, won't make eye contact, even," he said. "Dad asked me if I'd sold my car yet. Then he tells me they've hired a Korean guy to man the cash register. These are people who don't trust anybody with their cash and they've hired this stranger?"

He didn't have to say it. His parents were shamed by

Fulin's sudden notoriety. It would've been easier for Fulin to bear if he could claim one hundred percent innocence, but of course he couldn't. No one made him have cyber sex. Now what little hope he had of holding on to his old life had evaporated, thanks to the media.

Lennox squeezed his hand. Their waitress came over to the table with the coffee pot and offered a cup to Fulin. She squinted at Fulin like she was trying to place him. He didn't notice. Outside the rain ran in sheets down the window. The cafe was noisy with morning conversation and the rattle of dishes.

Channel 4 News came on the television over the bar with another exclusive about the Bauer murder. The television was set to closed captioning.

"That fucking Chrissy Nash," Lennox said in a low voice.

"What?" Fulin said, and turned in time to see his mug shot next to an innocent candid of Matilda Bauer projected on a screen behind Chrissy.

More evidence in the Matilda Bauer murder. A close neighbor has identified Matilda Bauer's parole officer, Fulin Chen, as having entered the Bauer house at noon on Sunday, March 5th, the approximate time at which Matilda Bauer died by what looked like autoerotic asphyxiation. No one else was seen entering or leaving the house.

She leaned forward and asked the camera:

Was this a deviant sex act that went too far, or was Matilda's murder the act of a jealous lover?

An old gal at the table next to them put her fork down on her plate and stared at Fulin, then waved the waitress down and asked her for a box and the check.

The whole room started buzzing, not in a friendly way.

"I got to get out of here," Fulin said. Maybe he was

being paranoid. Maybe they both were. Lennox slapped a five-dollar bill on the table for their coffee and they grabbed their coats, half expecting to get pelted with silverware. They made it to the street. Fulin pulled his collar up to hide his face. She told him to meet her at the office; she was going to find out more about this Chrissy Nash person.

• • •

It only took a few minutes to come up with a general bio. Chrissy had graduated from the University of Oregon with a double major in communications and broadcast journalism. She landed a television news job in Idaho Falls her first year out of school. Next stop, Bend, Oregon. Three years later she started working for Channel 4 in Portland. The woman had just turned thirty. So she was ambitious, big surprise. It was easy to know what she wanted: she wanted a big career. What was she scared of? Who did she hate? What did she hide from everybody? These were the kind of things that were hard to dig up from search engines, no matter how much you pay.

But Lennox spent some money on a deep search and came up with an interesting story from Chrissy's college days.

"Here's something," she told Fulin.

Back when Chrissy was a sophomore, she heard a few rumors that some frat boys were getting girls drunk and raping them. So Chrissy took it upon herself to go after Phi Beta Whatever.

"So she goes to this party," Lennox said. "It was after a game, the Ducks killed it, everybody happy, high, and already partying. Our girl Chrissy pretends to be a whole lot drunker than she is, and here's where the stories diverge:

She gets herself in a situation with three Greeks. Now they say it was totally one hundred percent her idea, but she writes a scathing story in the Emerald Media."

"Holy crap," Fulin said.

Exactly. One kid lost his scholarship over the incident. Another kid's folks threatened to sue the school, and Chrissy was forced to retract the story.

Somehow Chrissy was able to remain on the newspaper. Her advisor said that "She was an idealistic young woman perhaps overzealous in her pursuit of justice." Idealistic? Hadn't Nash's advisor heard of entrapment? What it said to Lennox was that Chrissy was a person who made up her mind about a story before she had all the facts. Lennox knew a cop like that; in fact she'd had a relationship with a cop like that.

She smelled Tommy all over this.

That sonuvabitch, Tommy, was the same kind of person as Chrissy. Made up his mind early in the investigation then gathered only the evidence that supported his version of the truth. He'd already been disciplined for disappearing evidence. He should have been fired. He was a man who lived by sleight of hand. Believe the trick and the trick stands.

"I'm thinking Pavlik's feeding her evidence," she said. "Chrissy's cute, probably willing to bed a source if it wins her a story." She picked up the phone. "Let's ask him how Chrissy's getting her inside information."

She dialed his cell number and held the phone out to Fulin.

It was the closest thing to a smile she'd seen on Fulin's face the whole morning. "You go ahead," he said. "You're a more experienced interrogator."

"Naw, this isn't interrogation," she said. "I'm just going

to chat him up."

Fulin's grin got a little wider.

Wider still when she punched the speakerphone button. The phone rang five times like Tommy was deciding whether to pick up or let it go to voicemail. On the seventh ring he answered.

"I'm working," he said.

"Of course you are," she said. "I could call you tonight at home."

"Our number's changed," he said.

"Uh huh." Like having an unlisted phone number was going to stop her. Who did he think he was dealing with?

"What do you want?" he said.

"I saw Chrissy Nash's news story this morning."

"Yeah?"

"Where's she getting her information?" Lennox said.

"She didn't get it from here," he told her. Even on the phone, she recognized his lying voice. She knew just what he was doing, twirling that hank of hair over his left ear.

Tommy said, "Nash probably canvassed the neighborhood and the witness told her."

"How could she possibly know that there were no other people seen entering the house other than the suspect who ID'd Fulin? That's privileged information, Tommy."

The phone went dead. She set it back on her desk. How could she have fallen in love with this guy? Thinking about it made her want to take a hot shower.

"He's playing with fire," she told Fulin. "Chrissy will make it impossible to get a fair trial in the state and the whole Portland justice system will look bad."

"But that doesn't clear my name," Fulin said.

The best thing for Fulin was to keep busy. "We need to

check out the Paulsons' financials," she said. "And see if you can find any of Debbie's client testimonials in Matilda's data. I'm going to look closer at Al Paulson. It's possible Debbie had an affair with Matilda and he found out about them."

Fulin's expression had changed now that he had a plan to move on. She knew the feeling. The only way to wrest yourself from Bad Luck's grip is to act. Not randomly, but with logical purpose. And if you were wrong, you backed up and rereasoned. Chance still overrode your efforts, but what other way did you have to combat chaos? A person can't sit on their ass and wait for Good Luck to walk by.

He was nodding, his expression, if not happy, purposeful. Lennox loved working with this guy. His work ethic, his love of research. Nothing was too boring or arcane for him to trace. He would make a hell of a partner if she could keep her hands off him.

CHAPTER 27

There's a whole lot of trouble you can tamp down during the day, but trouble has a way of coming back at you at night when you're trying to sleep. Lennox had the bad dream again and woke up on her feet, trying to catch her breath, the sheets twisted around her. It was three a.m. and raining.

She shrugged into a sweater, climbed down the stairs to check the locks again. A black BMW was parked on the curb in front of old lady Kurtz's house. Fulin's car. Lennox had said goodnight to him hours ago. She pulled on her boots and coat and unlocked her front door.

Outside the only sound was rain striking rooftops and pavement. The air smelled of wet fir trees and the cold had a bite to it. She ran over to Fulin's car, peered through the fogged up windows. There was a body curled in the back seat. She banged on the car window with the flat of her hand. He struggled in the blankets and sat up.

"Fulin," she shouted over the rain. He unlocked the door and pushed it open.

"What are you doing here?" she said.

He didn't answer. She watched him unfold his body and sit up. She couldn't read his face. Hell, it was the middle of the night and raining; what did she know?

"Come in the house," she said.

He followed her in. She put a kettle on for tea while he hunched wordlessly at the dining room table. She told him to make a fire; she'd fix sandwiches.

Fulin was sitting on his heels feeding sticks to keep the fire going when she brought in the food. He had surprisingly broad shoulders for such a slender man. His torso elegant, long, and sinewy. His braid swung down to his butt.

"Eat," she said.

He mumbled something.

"It's the middle of the night," she said. "Are you going to tell me what's going on or what."

He rocked back on his feet and stood up, turned to her. God in heaven he looked unhappy. "I'm sorry," he said.

"What are you doing sleeping in your car?"

He walked over to the sofa and sat next to her. He didn't say anything until she shook his arm and told him to talk, goddamn it.

"There's a movement at my condo to buy me out. A lot of the women don't feel safe. I take the stairs. If I use the elevator they all get off when I get on." He rubbed his knuckle across his mouth. "I'm the good guy. I help people get their lives back on track."

A tear squeezed out the corner of his eye and ran along the plane of his fine, satiny nose.

She remembered how it had been when she lost the trust of the people she worked with, her community. She had seen her lover bleeding out on that dusty back yard. Her partner's head blown apart. Shock after shock after shock.

Called in and questioned. Why did she put her partner in harm's way? Her fellow officers looking at her the same way she imagined the women in Fulin's condo looking at him. No one saw him as a good guy anymore. He was a person never to be trusted again.

Both of them thrown out of the garden for the rest of their lives. The slut and the wanker.

"Why don't you stay here," she said. It sounded good to her to say that. "I've got a guest room. We'll find out who killed Matilda and you can go back to your old life."

They both knew that wasn't happening. But Fulin laid his sandwich on his plate. "I've been thinking." He took a breath. "I'd make a pretty good detective."

She nodded. Absolutely.

"Cooper and Associates," he said. He grinned a crooked little grin. "With my reputation, I could be a real asset."

"Yeah, you could," she told him, at the same time not knowing where the revenue would come from to pay for an extra head. But damn, she was willing to go on faith or whatever the hell. What she didn't want to do was calculate the odds. Fuck the odds. She couldn't live exclusively on probabilities. She had a heart.

She showed him his room, showed him where the extra clean bath towel was stored, and told him goodnight.

• • •

She lay in bed for a long time, her mind churning through the facts of the Bauer murder. She made endless mental lists. Then suddenly, her mind touched on Miss Slocum's third grade class. It was Valentine's Day and Lennox found herself alone in the classroom. She raided her classmates' handmade mailboxes, stole their valentines and erased their names. Caitlin, Scotty, Tyson. She then readdressed them to herself and stuffed her mailbox to brimming.

Lennox had some sense of her bedroom door opening, but she couldn't shake the memory, the little white envelopes with "Lennox" written in her own cursive. The growing awareness of the class. One of her classmates had started to cry. Miss Slocum stood over Lennox's desk. She asked to see Lennox's valentines. Lennox was so busted. Her teacher had that look, the one where she had high hopes for Lennox, but Lennox had proved herself a low creature.

She didn't hear Fulin cross the room, but she felt his body as he eased his weight alongside her. He didn't slip under the covers, but stayed chastely on top of the bed. His breath slowed and grew regular. Lennox relaxed and fell asleep.

CHAPTER 28

Fulin delved deeper into the Paulsons' financials to find that Debbie Paulson was making most of the money in the family. When Alfa Romeo stopped selling cars in the U.S., Al Paulson was left without a dealership. Paulson's Imports became a strictly repair business, and he wasn't a mechanic. His income shrank by half. Al still owned the shop, paid the rent, the taxes, and made payroll. Then two years ago, his shop got in trouble over a compliance issue. He had to hire a big-name legal firm to keep him from losing everything. But he still raced his Alfa on a circuit that ran from southern California to Idaho, leaving Debbie to shoulder their big honking mortgage payment.

Lennox had taken a good look at Debbie; now it was time to check out the husband. The mechanic at Paulson's Imports told her she could find him at PIR.

PIR, Portland International Raceway, was located in the north part of town on what was once known as Vanport, a floodplain wedged just beyond the north city boundary and the Columbia River. The city of Vanport had been built to house the shipyard workers during World War II and boasted a population of 40,000 souls, nearly half of them black Americans. After the war, the population dropped by half.

Back in those days, Portland was home to many Ku Klux Klan members, and was called "a northern city with southern sensibilities." After the war, many of Portland's civic leaders invited Vanport's blacks to go back to where they came from. The blacks ignored their invitation. In 1948, nature accomplished what the city leaders failed to do. The Columbia River rose fifteen feet, punching a hole in the dike that protected Vanport from flooding. The river killed fifteen people and washed away the city. Portland bought the property in 1960, dozed it, and built a racetrack.

Lennox hadn't been out at PIR since she'd worked in vice years ago. The neighborhood was just the way she remembered: flat as a tabletop, covered in scrubby grass, and without a fir or cedar tree in sight. The track itself ran just under two miles in length, stretched and folded to give the racers and their fans many opportunities to appreciate disaster.

She parked the Bronco by the pit area and walked to the main grandstand. Close to sixty people huddled in groups of two to six, spreading themselves across bleachers that could hold thousands of people during Indy races. Lennox went to the far end of the stand over by Turn Two to watch the race. A yellow Porsche swung across the track, blocking the Alfa from passing in the turn behind him. When the two cars made the turn, a black Jag shot from behind and overtook both of them. The announcer called Larry Butler in the lead. The rest of the cars followed clustered in a tight pack. The cars went around the track three more times,

Butler never losing the front position. An older woman waved the checkered flag. Larry Butler's Jag placed first, followed by Al Paulson's Alfa, in second, followed by the yellow Porsche.

After the race, Lennox found Al trailering his Alfa. She stood by the ramp and waited for him to climb out of the trailer. Al stood six foot and lanky, dressed in a tee shirt and the trousers end of a one-piece race suit, the top half flopping behind him. He looked to have a silver buzz cut under his red Alfa cap. The way he looked at her made her feel that she was trespassing.

"Congratulations on the second," she said. "But you were robbed."

"That's racing," he said. His tone was guarded but polite. "What can I do for you?"

She showed him her license. "I'm investigating the Matilda Bauer murder," she said.

"Who told you I was here?"

"I'm a detective," she said. "Did you know Matilda Bauer?"

"The kinky chick that got herself killed," he said. "Lady, I never met the woman. And I'm tired. I can't tell you a thing that I didn't hear about on the news." He slid the lip of the handcart under his tool chest and rolled it back up the ramp into the trailer. He jumped the four feet from the trailer floor to the pavement and started collapsing the four lawn chairs in his pit, ignoring her.

"Your wife was a good friend of Matilda Bauer's," she said.

He stopped loading and looked at her in disbelief. "That's impossible. I know my wife's friends. There are no sex workers in my wife's crowd." he said.

"She never mentioned a Mattie or Matilda?"

"You've got the wrong person," he said. "I know Debbie's friends. They're like Debbie."

He looked like he was telling the truth.

"Where were you on the weekend of March 4th?" she said.

He thought for a minute. "There was a race in Spokane," he said. "I left Friday."

"Can you verify that?" Lennox said.

"Sure. Mike O'Connor officiated. He runs the Spokane chapter."

"And what time did you get home?" she said.

"Sunday. I don't know. Five o'clock, I guess."

Debbie had told Lennox the two of them had gone to church, had breakfast in town. Debbie's alibi was so busted. She could've been Matilda's partner, leaking local contacts that Matilda seduced and squeezed money from. She could've been Matilda's lover with the same motive as Joey.

"Did Debbie seem to be her regular self?" she said.

A shadow passed across his face. Nothing for sure, but Lennox guessed he was rethinking his recent home life. He said, "Do we need to hire a lawyer?"

"You didn't notice that she was depressed, or anything like that?"

There was something there, something he wasn't telling Lennox.

"Matilda Bauer was with Debbie at your house until late Saturday," Lennox said. "Your wife was probably the last person other than the murderer to see Matilda Bauer alive."

"Let me see your license again."

The time it took her to dig out her license and show it to him gave him enough space to think. He pulled himself taller and said, "You got the wrong Debbie."

• • •

Al looked in no mood to hoist a glass with his friends and kibitz about the race. Lennox was betting that Al planned on heading straight home from the pits, which gave her a half hour tops to drive to the Paulson estate and see if she could wangle the truth out of Debbie.

Debbie answered the door on the third ring. "You!" she said. Her pupils were still dilated, but her facial muscles were tauter, and she was dressed up in black capris, a white silk tunic, and jeweled sandals. Something like a pot roast smell was wafting into the foyer and out the front door.

"That's right, Lennox Cooper." Lennox handed her business card to Debbie. "I figure we have maybe twenty minutes before Al gets home. Heads up, he didn't look very happy. He lost that last heat to this joker who blocked him. Guess that's racing."

Debbie blinked twice. "You met with my husband?"

"Yup." Lennox said. "Are you going to let me in?"

"Why did you do that?" she said. "Who told you you could do that?"

"Look lady," Lennox said. "You told a big whopping lie about Sunday. Your alibi was up in Spokane the morning Matilda was murdered."

Debbie opened the door wider and led Lennox to the same floral sofa as her last interview.

Lennox looked at her watch. "You have fifteen minutes."

Debbie twisted her fingers, twisted her wedding ring like she was trying to pull it off, but it was stuck on there good. It took her another couple minutes before she made up her mind. "Mattie left Saturday around three, maybe later, I can't remember. I started drinking. Crying. I got wasted. I woke up around noon the next morning. I'd gotten sick on myself, on the upholstery. The whole living room smelled like vomit. Al due back around five and I couldn't even stand up without getting sick."

"Why did Mattie leave?"

"I told her I'd sell my client base, get divorced. We could move anywhere she wanted; she could change her identity. And I'd start a new business, maybe call it Covenant or Harmony. In another state, she could be my partner."

"She didn't go for it."

Debbie shook her head, still wringing her hands. She had her wedding ring twisted halfway over her knuckle.

Lennox sagged into the sofa cushion. All the sorrows a life can throw your way, death of your hopes was the worst bitch of all.

"I was passed out when Matilda was murdered," Debbie said.

And man, she sold it. Sure as sure, Lennox was looking at a woman with a broken heart. A broken heart and no alibi.

Lennox stood and headed for the front door. She turned to say goodbye. "Keep my card," Lennox said. "In case you think of anything Mattie might have said that can give us a lead."

Debbie nodded and thanked her. Thanked her for what? Believing her story, or getting the hell out of there before her husband got home?

Lennox could believe her story all day long. Bottom line, the woman didn't have an alibi.

CHAPTER 29

Now that Fulin had been indicted, Chrissy Nash at Channel 4 News dropped the angle of autoerotic asphyxiation and moved on to men in positions of authority taking advantage of disadvantaged women. She interviewed Bradley Comfort, the TV shrink, who spoke at length about how teachers, CEOs, and even cops and prison guards use their power over the women they supervise.

The news played from eight o'clock until nine in the morning and then back at six in the evening. Lennox figured the best time to reach Chrissy was after the morning news hour. But you might as well try to break into a jail as get in the front door of KOPD, Channel 4. The place was even built like a prison: windowless cement, and completely unadorned. The entrance opened in the back of the building.

Lennox walked up to the entry. The sign next to a telephone said call and state your business. Through the glass entrance Lennox saw a stick thin woman with yellow spikes for hair sitting behind a counter. She was dressed entirely in black.

Lennox picked up the phone. "I'm here to see Chrissy Nash."

"Do you have an appointment?" the woman said.

"No, but she'll want to see me," Lennox said. "It's about the Fulin Chen case."

"Name?" the receptionist said.

Lennox gave it to her. The receptionist pushed a button on her phone and spoke, then her face hardened. She nodded and hung up the phone.

"Ms. Nash only sees people who have appointments."

"May I make an appointment?"

The communication slid downhill from there. So fine. It wasn't the first gated community she'd penetrated. She went home and did a little research. Discovered that three days a week Channel 4 invited in a live audience for their *Good Morning Portland* show. The next morning Lennox dressed in a skirt and jacket, three-inch heels, and round glasses. She wore her hair down. She even used hot curlers. And she got in.

The inside of the station was only slightly less utilitarian than the outside of the building. Old carpet, white cement block walls, a lit awards case with eight awards spread across the four glass shelves.

The television audience thing was complete hooey. The audience sat in a glass-fronted room watching a large television screen while the TV hosts filmed in a studio in another part of the building. Lennox took an aisle seat and looked around. All the people in the audience looked to be wearing audition clothes. She saw a man check his teeth with a small hand mirror he'd pulled out of his pocket. Several people smoothed their hair. Their clothes. After everyone was seated, a TV person came in and showed them the electronic sign that lit when it was time to laugh or clap.

Lennox gave herself five minutes after the TV person left, then she slipped out to use the facilities. She pulled a clipboard and some typed sheets from her bag. The hall was empty.

Lennox tried a few doors. She poked her head in the production studio. The room was dark with five screens lit up on the far wall. She asked for Chrissy Nash. A production guy looked up from the console and told her to try the dressing room, first door to the right. Lennox tapped softly on the door and opened it. Chrissy sat in front of a mirror outlined in lights, wiping a half-inch of makeup off her face. She wore a bib over her black sweater. There were no vases of flowers, no assistants, no silks and jewelry like you see in the movies. It looked more like a bathroom in a convenience store without the toilet and sink.

Lennox flipped her detective license in front of Chrissy. "I'd like to talk about Fulin Chen," she said.

Chrissy swiveled in her chair to look Lennox in the eye. A long streak of pale skin on her forehead was exposed from the orange makeup. "Are you working on his defense team? Or did he assault you?"

"The evidence against Fulin is circumstantial," Lennox said. "You're ruining his ability to work or even live in this city."

Chrissy grabbed a stack of cotton pads, dipped them in oil and started removing her eye makeup. "The evidence is not just circumstantial. There are the hairs and the eyewitness."

"How do you know about the hair?" Lennox said.

"I have a reliable source."

"When we prove that Fulin is innocent, you will be

liable for his loss of reputation," Lennox said.

Chrissy stared at her from the mirror. Her naked face was flawless, her features uniform and uninteresting, like those popular girls in high school, a time when everyone tried to look like the same fashion model. "He's a pervert," Chrissy said. Her chin tipped up, the picture of self-righteousness. "And I didn't ruin his career. He did that to himself. I saw the pictures."

How in God's name did Chrissy come across those photos? They were in an evidence locker. "Chrissy, who's giving you access to police evidence?"

"I don't have to talk to you," Chrissy said. "I don't even know how you got in here."

"Tommy Pavlik?" Lennox said. And watched Chrissy's reflection for tells. Yup. She flipped her hair like she was still in grade school. Lennox waited for her to say something like "Fiddle-de-de." But she didn't. It was Tommy, the bastard.

"You better watch yourself. Fulin's attorney is already looking into suing you for defamation of character."

"I've run my stories past legal." Chrissy gave her hair another flip.

* * *

When Lennox got back to the office, Fulin was hard at work building a spreadsheet of all Matilda's internet "friends," including the imaginary ones she used to build credible identities.

"You left early this morning," he said.

She told him that she'd met with Chrissy Nash. "Tommy's feeding her information," she said.

Fulin listened, the muscle underneath his jaw working.

"I guess there's no way to stop her," he said.

"We'll stop her," she said. "And we'll find the killer."

"Somebody vandalized your house last night," he said. "There was red sticky shit on the siding and all over the porch floor. At first I thought it was blood."

"God," she said. She'd left by the back door this morning. She started for the basement to get the scrub bucket.

"I already cleaned it up," Fulin said. "You're acting like this isn't the first time."

"My old partner, John Doran?"

Fulin nodded.

"His kid."

"Why?"

"Because somebody must've told him I was responsible for John's death," she said.

"That's bullshit," Fulin said. "John wasn't your fault. You saved Tommy's life, John saved yours."

"I didn't follow police procedure."

"If you'd done that, Tommy would've likely died," Fulin said. "How many times has the kid been over here?"

"Eight?" she said. "It's mostly the fake blood."

"You've got to go the cops," Fulin said.

"And tell them their dead comrade's kid is harassing me?"

"You're saying you can't put a stop to this?" Fulin said.

Lennox stared down at her shoes. Fulin could tell her a thousand times it wasn't her fault, she'd still feel the weight of John's death on her heart.

Fulin took her hand between both of his and made sure she looked straight at him. "You're not doing that kid any favors," he said. "He can't grow up thinking it's okay to act out. That was the deal with all my clients. They started acting out as kids. Sometimes they'd get away with it. But then they don't get away with it and they end up in jail. You've got to set this kid straight."

"How do I do that? What do I say?"

"Tell him his father was a hero," Fulin said. "He saved your life when you pulled your fellow officer behind cover. That what he's doing makes his whole family look bad."

Could Lennox say that to Cory? Look him in the eye without guilt?

Not yet.

CHAPTER 30

The way Lennox saw it, there were three possible motives for killing Matilda Bauer. Blackmail, which pointed squarely at Hobby Glover. But murder using autoerotic asphyxiation was a big step past spanking on a fantasy web site. And the bruising on Matilda's legs indicated her murderer grabbed her by the thighs and made sure she never regained her footing. Glover didn't seem like the kind of guy who could wrestle anything bigger than an eleven-year-old to the ground. Could he manhandle a grown woman? Sure, if she was choking to death at the time. There was the problem of alibi, as he had one that looked pretty solid.

Then there was the jealous lover motive, making either Joey Tufts or Debbie Paulson chief suspect. Joey was absolutely capable of losing his head and killing Matilda, but why the S&M angle? Did he catch her with a lover and just lose it? Then where was the lover? Debbie had no alibi. What if she discovered she'd been betrayed? How would she react?

Hold on. What if Debbie was the lover Joey found with

Matilda? Lennox found herself loving that idea.

But there was the third possible motive: a partnership that had turned sour. Matilda was incorrigible; everything Lennox had learned pointed to it. How do you partner with someone who takes insane risks? Eliminating the partnership pointed to Debbie Paulson, Joan Strake and Emily Cross.

It was late in the afternoon, Lennox so deep in the data files she hadn't noticed how dark it had grown outside. A flash ignited the southeast sky followed by a crack of thunder that startled her. Lightning storms in Portland were rare as snowfall, and as exciting. Lennox stood up, stretched her back and went into the kitchen for a mug of tea. The rain came down in force now, pounding on her roof. Another flash of lightning lit up the kitchen windows, followed immediately with a giant crack of thunder.

She heard the front door slam and found Fulin in the living room, shedding his leather jacket and boots. His look was as sour as his body was wet. He gave her a half wave and stomped across the room, down the hall to the guest room and closed the door behind him. She added a mug and set out the tray on the sofa table, waiting.

A few minutes later he came out in dry clothes, his expression resolute. He sank into the easy chair across from her. The rain slammed against her living room windows.

"Bad meeting with your folks?" she said.

He took a sip of tea, made a face and put the cup back on the table. "Could I have a real drink?"

She went back to the kitchen and fetched up the Jack Daniels and two glasses of ice. She let him pour his own.

He near filled his glass and said, "All the shit the media is saying about me, my face smeared everywhere, I can't even live in my own house, and what do the folks want to talk about? Dry cleaning. How I can take over their business. If I took over the business I could afford to keep my car and pay them back for my legal fees. Now all of the sudden they want to move to Florida."

Fulin shuddered. Took a long pull from his glass and shuddered again.

"I can't do it. I just can't."

Two short years ago Lennox had a similar come-to-Jesus with her mother about what to do now that her career was down the toilet. All those years of training and working and gaining experience, taking on the identity of the job. *I'm a cop. This is how I think, feel, and act.* Then it's gone, and you barely recognize your own face in the mirror.

It was her turn to shudder. She poured herself a thimble of whiskey and sipped it.

"I want to work for you," Fulin said. "Not just my case, but all the time. You know, Lennox Cooper and Associates. I'm good at this and I can help drum up business. Hell, the whole Chinese community could be coming to us for help."

She tried to say something, but he talked over the top of her. He said, "I'd be an assistant at first. I'm fine with that. You know I'm good with computers and paperwork."

He put his drink down and leaned forward so that his knees were touching hers. "Before? Babysitting ex-felons, making sure they showed up for work, kept to their AA meetings. Nine times out of ten, they'd blow it. What I've been doing for you? Running surveillance, and tracking leads? It's like I'm doing something with a purpose."

He loved her business. Imagine that. All this time she'd been moaning to herself about what she'd lost when she'd been fired. Beginning with no freaking respect. Nowadays she was a plain citizen, make that *female* citizen. No, make that *small, female citizen*. Witnesses didn't have to talk to her unless they felt like it. And if they did talk to her they could lie their asses off. It was not against the law. And you could bet your butt if she was still a cop no pissed-off teenagers would be splashing fake blood all over her house.

"You're your own boss," Fulin said. "You decide your own priorities, make your own schedule. You don't have to put up with the political crap."

"Fulin, I barely make my mortgage. I can't afford an employee."

But jeez, she'd love to have Chen work for her. They were a great team. She loved the company. That was something she missed about being a cop. She was so freaking alone.

Fulin had jumped from his chair and waved his arms at her.

"I'll work for free. Like now," Fulin said. He shook his head when he saw her reaction. "No. I'll sell my condo. If I have to, I'll sell my car. That'll give us a little financial room. And I'll put the word out with the Chinese community."

She'd love to take him on. In time, a partner. She grinned before she knew she was grinning. And toasted him. "Let me think about it."

The doorbell rang. Frank at the door in the rain. And shit! They had dinner reservations, and she was dressed in sweats, looking like she'd rolled out of bed and worked all day that way. Which she had.

"Frank, I'm sorry, I lost track of time. I can be ready in ten. Make yourself a drink." She turned to Fulin. "Would you get Frank some ice? Thanks."

"Ten!" she shouted over her shoulder and bounded up the stairs, trying not to invest too much thought in the look on Frank's face when he took in Lennox and Fulin clicking whiskey glasses together. She could explain at dinner.

She stripped out of her sweats, rolled on some antiperspirant and wiggled into a low cut top. Her best designer jeans, stilettos. Then teeth, a good face scrub, moisturizer, hair, eye pencil, lipstick. God, it took forever to be a girl.

Four minutes late. With luck and a little whiskey, Frank would've rearranged his face. That confusion, disappointment, and maybe a little shard of hurt would be gone. It sucks to have the guy you're sleeping with look at you like that.

"I'm ready," she said.

Gone disappointment. Hello attentive. Impressed.

Frank set his mostly finished drink on the table. "Give me a minute, I need to use the bathroom."

He walked down the hall, and then halted. Halted and came back to where Lennox was standing by the coat closet. "Is Chen living here?" he said.

Fulin hoisted himself out of the easy chair. "It's platonic, man. I'm just working for Lennox here, and my condo thing is kind of fucked up. It's just for a short time." He spread his arms in a gesture, showing empty. Nada. "Lennox and me, we're strictly professional."

She said, "We're late. Let's have dinner and I'll explain."

Explain again.

Lennox hooked her coated arm in Frank's and met some resistance, which pissed her off. Since when did she have to do so much damn explaining? Her business, her hours, her friendships.

They managed to leave and run through the rain to Frank's car. And even in the rain and even though he was pissed at her, he ran to her side and unlocked her door first. He was a thoughtful man. He unlocked his door and flopped into the driver's seat.

He stared forward through the rain-sheeted windshield. "I don't think I can do this," he said.

"What do you mean 'this', Frank?"

"Half the time, no, two-thirds of the time I ask you out and you can't," he said. "You've got to work. You're always working. And it's all about Fulin. Fulin this and Fulin that and I've got to run help Fulin. Now the guy is living with you?"

Lennox placed her hand on his arm. Felt his muscles through the coat. "He's staying with me, not living, but let's forget that piece for one minute. The rest of what you're talking about is my work," she said. "It has weird hours and I can't help that. The Fulin, Fulin, Fulin stuff, that's just my obsession with the case. He's my client."

She shifted her body so that she faced his profile. "Look at me," she said. She tipped his chin gently towards her.

"He's also a friend," she said. "You don't know what it feels like to lose everything you've been working for, everything you've become. I do."

Frank looked at her like he was trying to read her. If Lennox was betting his face, she'd know there was no way she was going to win this hand. There was a lot that was a shame about that.

CHAPTER 31

Lennox lay in bed, listening to the rain pound her roof and willing herself to sleep. Thinking about Frank, thinking they never had a chance. Did they? She wasn't an easy woman to love. It seemed like the only men that had loved her were so deeply flawed that she never could make a go of it with them. Rehashing her love affairs, one-night stands. Their flaws, her flaws. The rain pounded overhead.

The rain stopped at 3:45. She must've dozed off after that. Next thing she knew the alarm screamed seven o'clock.

Lennox bent down to retrieve her morning paper when the Channel 4 news van pulled up to the curb of her house. The van door slid back and two men, a cameraman and a cord and cable guy, debarked making their way along her sidewalk, followed by Chrissy Nash. Chrissy Nash all made up for television, in a crisp raincoat, black trousers and ankle boots. Lennox in her pajamas, barefoot, hair sleep mussed.

Chrissy took the lead, microphone in hand, cordman trailing, cameraman bringing up the rear. Lennox rushed down the porch steps to block Chrissy from getting any closer to her house.

"Private property, Chrissy. I want you people off my sidewalk, pronto."

Chrissy snapped her fingers at the cameraman and made a rolling motion with her hand. The cameraman gave an order to cable-guy, who fetched up a distance lens.

"Back!" Lennox ordered using her low register cop voice. Standing toe to toe with Chrissy, Lennox forced the newswoman backwards until they reached the sidewalk.

Nose to nose with Chrissy Nash until Nash was able to wrestle the microphone up to her mouth.

"We are at the residence of Lennox Cooper, who is believed to be harboring murder suspect Fulin Chen. Ms. Cooper, a former policewoman and former girlfriend of Mr. Chen's is working on Mr. Chen's defense team."

Two simple sentences, a helix of lie and truth impossible to defend oneself against. Especially in pajamas. The wise course was to retreat. Fuck that.

"You've twisted some evidence that you could have only gotten from one source," Lennox said. "Once I can prove it, your insider will be charged. There are laws against what you've been doing. I hope you enjoy litigation, lady." Lennox turned on her heel and marched up the steps into her house.

"We have questions for Mr. Chen," Chrissy's raised voice called from behind her.

Lennox opened her front door. Chrissy made a crazy dash up the sidewalk to the bottom step of the porch before Lennox was able to slam it in her face.

"Fulin Chen, we know you're in there," Chrissy shouted through the door.

Down the hall, Fulin stepped out of his bedroom in a

tee shirt and boxers. "What's up?" he said sleepily.

"Get back in your room," Lennox said in a harsh whisper.

She reclosed the brown velvet curtains across her living room and dining room windows. The rooms retreated into heavy twilight. She dashed into the kitchen.

Only when the main floor was covered from outside view did she return to the kitchen and pour herself a mug of coffee. She drank it scalding. She wanted to rip Chrissy's smug goddamn face off, tear her carefully highlighted hair out by its roots. Not only was Fulin's career demolished, but thanks to Chrissy, it was unlikely that he could have any kind of a life in Portland. And it was all in a day's work for that heartless, lying bitch.

Fulin walked into the kitchen. He had slipped into his jeans. "What the hell?" he said.

She told him how Chrissy had paid them a visit with her camera crew, describing Lennox on tape as "former girlfriend harboring a murder suspect."

Fulin's frame sagged against the kitchen counter. He dragged his hand over his downturned mouth.

It was dead quiet in the kitchen. No hint from outside that Chrissy and crew were still there, just the occasional burp from the coffee maker.

"I've dragged you down with me," Fulin said.

"Bullshit." Her reputation was way spotty before she'd ever agreed to take on his case. But yes, thanks to Chrissy, Lennox was getting even more notoriety. "Former girlfriend," on local news, what was Frank going to make of that? What was the judge going to make of it when they went to trial? She was so freaking sick of people and their shitty assumptions about her character.

"How did Chrissy know that you're staying here?"

Lennox said. "How does she know that we're friends? It's not like any of that's public information."

Fulin shrugged. "Anyone from the district attorney's office could've told her, anybody from the cop shop."

"Tommy," she said. "It's Tommy that's been feeding her information from the beginning."

"We can't prove it," Fulin said.

"The hell we can't. I'm going to make it my second priority after proving you're innocent in this train wreck of a case." Train wreck came out of her mouth before she could swallow it back. He flinched as soon as she said it.

"I'm going to have to move to another state where they've never heard of me," he said.

Just him saying it, she felt her world shrink. She realized in that moment she couldn't let him disappear from her life if she had any power at all.

"You can't," she said. "You're going to work for me. Cooper and Associates." She poured herself another cup of coffee and then it occurred to her.

"You know, Chrissy Nash could be a blessing in disguise."

"That's not possible," he said.

"We prove you're innocent. Net result? All that media coverage turns into the kind of public relations we could've never afforded. Looking for a private investigator? Cooper and Associates: that rings a bell."

Fulin shook his head. "Sure, and people will always look at me and be reminded of Matilda Bauer, and how she died. I don't think I can live with that."

How to explain to him that time builds scar tissue. Finding your own integrity in the face of a whole lot of people thinking you're lower than dirt changes you, makes you tougher than you thought possible. And those people who still care about you and stand behind you? They're more precious than rubies.

"I won't let you down," she said.

She walked to the dining room and peeked through the heavy drapes out on the street, Fulin on her heels. The Channel 4 truck had left.

She opened the front door very slowly, in case Chrissy and her minions were hiding in the shrubbery. They were not.

"Where are you going?" he said.

"I'm getting my morning paper."

CHAPTER 32

It had just stopped raining. Lennox gave her umbrella a shake and stepped into the Shanty Bar and Grill. The cops lining the bar stools sat cheek to cheek drinking beer and watching "Dancing with the Stars." Most of them glanced at the door as she entered; a few of them gave her a friendly nod. Except for this one cop sitting next to Fish.

"Where's The Pervert?" he said, in a voice that carried over the television and the barroom chitchat.

"Do I know you?" she said.

She didn't. He looked to be in his late thirties, sandy hair, on the stocky side. The cop smirked like he was Mr. Comedy, which was about the time that Fish's elbow caught the man's drinking arm. Sent beer splashing on the bar and down the cop's shirt.

"Sorry, man," Fish said. He swiped at the guy's front as he tipped his beer so that it splashed over the cop's shoes. A couple of other cops caught the action, and chuckled.

And what could Mr. Comedy do? Take a swing at Fish? Fish outranked him.

"Let me buy you the next one," Fish said, his voice faux-apologetic. He slapped a five-dollar bill on the bar and stood up.

"Come on Cooper, let's play some cards," he said.

She was liking old Fish so much it was hard to believe that two short years ago they were enemies. They walked past a row of tables, the locals spooning chowder and munching on garlic bread. Everyone drinking beer, everyone talking and laughing and enjoying their Friday night.

Ham, Jerry, and Sarge were seated at the table when Fish opened the door to the back room, Ham shuffling the cards on the stained green felt, Jerry stacking up the poker chips.

Jerry did a double take when he saw her walk in with Fish. "Where's Chen?" he said.

"He's having dinner with his folks," Lennox said.

"On poker night?" Ham said.

"They want him to take over the dry cleaning business."

Fish snorted. Then realized no one else was laughing.

"He's not going back into law enforcement," Sarge said.

"Sure," Jerry said. "But I don't see Fulin spending his life Martinizing."

"Where's Frank?" Lennox said, figuring the answer and dreading it.

Ham shook his head. The kind of headshake that said Frank wasn't coming back.

"Shit, Cooper," Fish said. "What did you do to him?"

"We kind of dumped each other."

"Damn," Fish said. "I liked him." Everyone looked disappointed and regretful, her most of all. It was still so fresh: his hands on her, the way he kissed, reading the newspapers in the morning, and how he interrupted her every five minutes with news from the national section while she was trying to read the metro section. It was like something old married people would do. In that moment, all she wanted to do was call him and beg forgiveness for being who she was.

"Are we going to play cards or what?" Sarge said. "My horoscope said I was coming into some money today."

"You read the horoscope?" Lennox said.

"It's in the stars," Ham said, and gave the cards one last shuffle. Lennox won the deal and dealt two cards down. She waited for everyone to check out their hand and then peeked. There was a whole lot Lennox did and didn't do in a life of courting Mr. Luck, and being last to peek was at the top of her list. Tonight he was smiling down on her head: a pair of sixes.

Sarge threw in two chips. Fish followed with an extra chip; the rest of the table passed. Lennox dealt the flop: queen, seven, and thank you, Mr. Luck, a six.

Sarge threw in a chip, Ham folded, and Lennox saw the bet. Ham dealt the turn card. A deuce.

Sarge, looking a whole lot more brave than lucky, raised another three; Jerry bumped it three. " I can't see it," he said. "Fulin and dry cleaning."

"He's going to work for me," she said.

Ham shook his head at what he obviously thought was Lennox's latest bit of foolishness.

"Raise three," she said. And damn if she didn't sound defiant. Sarge and Jerry hung in there as she swept the pot. All those juicy chips didn't make her feel any less defensive.

Katy, the cocktailer, poked her head in the door. "Anyone for a beverage?" she said.

"Jack and coke," Lennox said.

"What about Fulin's case?" Jerry said.

"Five suspects," Lennox said. "And I got some solid info this afternoon."

"But the plan was," Ham said, "you get enough ahead that you rent office space instead of having everyone in the world come through your front door. Then employees."

"Sure. And Fulin can press trousers," she said.

"It's a security thing," Ham said. "Bad enough if you were a big guy, but you're not."

She hadn't even told Ham about Cory Doran. She didn't want the load of spiel about how it wasn't her fault. How she had to deal with the kid and put an end to it.

"It's your deal," Sarge said to Jerry.

They played a couple more hours, Lennox winning more pots than not, which figured. Lucky in cards, unlucky in love. Ham questioning her judgment. Fuck it, she'd have another Jack and coke. She was walking home, who cared if she was a little wobbly. How's that for judgment?

At the end of the night, poor Sarge ended ninety-two bucks down. So much for the stars.

The bar had emptied of cops and was replaced by one elderly lady bending the bartender's ear. An old Nirvana tune played on the jukebox. A couple of tables of twenty-somethings were drinking pitchers. The place smelled less of fried fish and more of spilled beer.

"Let me give you a ride home," Ham said to her.

Like she needed more advice from good old Ham. "Thanks anyway," she said. "I need to walk off the buzz."

"But—" he said.

"C'mon Ham." Jerry swung an arm around Ham's shoulder. "She's a big girl with a twenty-minute walk in a safe neighborhood."

Ham looked like he wanted to argue the point, then thought better of it. She waved goodbye to them and to Sarge and Fish, who'd both taken a seat at the bar some stools away from the old lady.

It smelled clean and ferny outside, and cold enough to lift the sludge from sitting on her backside drinking whiskey for three hours in french-fried air. A light drizzle swept the sidewalk. She put up her umbrella and crossed Forty-seventh, walking the two blocks to Broadway. Even though it was Friday night and not quite midnight, most of the houses she passed were dark, save the porch lights.

There was no point getting in a snit about Ham. Ham had always been worried about her finances. Back in college he'd worried about them, and thank God somebody had. It was true what he said about having her office in her house. It maybe wouldn't stop Cory Doran from splashing fake blood over her porch, but it'd make it harder for the likes of Joey Tufts to break in and assault her.

She tripped where the sidewalk buckled from a tree root and fell to one knee. Her umbrella jerked from her hand and bounced on the wet sidewalk. Taking a fall, even a little one, has a way of shaking you up, making you take notice. Like, look at her, half in the bag, thinking about renting and not watching where she was going. Forty-sixth and Broadway; six short blocks and she was home free.

The drizzle escalated to a hard rain. It bounced off her umbrella and soaked her boots. She walked faster, with her head down, the umbrella up by her face like a shield. She reached the corner of her rock garden.

And got knocked to the ground. A man pinned her arms over her head. She struggled against him and screamed help for all she was worth. He punched her in the ribs. He pulled her up by her hair. She twisted and tried to kick him. He punched her in the kidneys. It took her breath away. He marched her up the stairs leading to her porch crooning obscenities into her ear. What a bitch she was, how she totally had this coming. She'd never seen this guy before. And truthfully? At this point, she quit giving him much of a fight. She was thinking, though.

They got to her front door. He dumped the contents of her bag on the porch floor and handed Lennox her keys.

"Help!" she screamed.

He punched her in the mouth. Hard enough she felt a crown loosen.

"Open the fucking door," he demanded.

Her closest weapon was in her desk. Old Ugly, her service revolver. She wasn't going to outrun this dude. Okay, submit. Then go for the kick, bite off his ear, whatever became available. But he didn't let her face him. He pushed her to the floor in front of the door and snapped a pair of cuffs around her wrists, a metallic clicking noise, and her arms were pinned behind her.

Once she was cuffed, he turned her over. The only light came from the kitchen, enough to see that he had dark eyes, dark hair, a mustache. She pegged him at one-ninety, five eleven. He tore her fleece open and broke the clasp on her bra.

"You want it rough, don't you darlin'?" he said.

She squirmed her body from side to side, thinking she still had her knees. Waiting for the moment when she could disable him.

Someone was climbing her porch steps. Fulin coming home. The sound of someone outside distracted her assailant long enough for Lennox to absolutely nail the guy's boner. With luck, it would crack in half and fall off. He fell off her and curled up on the floor, gasping for breath.

Fulin pushed the door open.

One look at Lennox's bloodied mouth, her torn clothes, and he pulled her attacker's head off the floor and blasted him in the face. Hit him again, and the guy's head lolled back.

"Handcuff keys," she said.

Fulin fished the dude's keys from his jacket pocket, uncuffed Lennox, and cuffed the assailant. His eyes fluttered open.

"Get his ID," she said.

Michael O'Reilly.

Lennox wrapped herself in a blanket and retrieved her cell from the porch floor. Called 911 and gave her information to the dispatch woman.

"I want to report an assault, attempted rape," she said. "His name is Michael O'Reilly."

Her attacker protested. "You can't do that. You invited me here."

"What the hell is he talking about?" Fulin said.

"We have him," Lennox said to the dispatch lady.

"How do you think I got your address, you cunt," he said. "You tricked me."

Lennox signed off with the dispatcher. She walked over to the man, hauled off and kicked him. She missed his kneecap by a couple inches, but still it was a good kick.

"I hate the "C" word," she said.

He yelled and then blubbered like a little kid. Told her she'd busted his leg.

"What are you talking about, I gave you my address?"

"Force.net," he said. "You've been advertising how

you like to be beaten and raped. I'll tell the cops, how you lured me—"

"I don't know what you're talking about," she said.

"It's a dating site for people who like it rough," he said. "I can show the police the site. I can show them your picture."

Lennox was too hurt, too scared to take him seriously. "Good luck with that," she said.

CHAPTER 33

After Lennox had been beaten and nearly raped, it was Fulin who worked all night to track the man who had set Lennox up for the assault. He found chat rooms where men who loved beating on women could connect with women who loved being beat. Someone had posted Lennox's identity and address on Force.net announcing she loved being raped. That someone was Hobby Glover. The internet address matched other postings with Glover's user name.

Hobby Fucking Glover. Why would he do this to her? To hurt her bad enough she wouldn't be able to continue the investigation? Lennox wondered if he'd pulled something like this with Matilda. He could've set her up in a bondage scenario with some crazy who took it too far.

She gave Fulin his first surveillance job: tail Glover every day after school. Turned out Mr. Vice Principal was on some kind of fitness plan. He had one of those step counter things you attach to your belt, and every day he drove to Forest Park for a hike in the woods. Every day for thirty minutes, Fulin said.

Forest Park. Right in the heart of Portland, it was a sprawling mass of wilderness crisscrossed with paths and creeks and what all. And huge. 4,800 acres of woods. All kinds of places to have a friendly, uninterrupted chat if you were willing to hike far enough in.

• • •

Pink blossoms scattered across the front lawn of Cedar Hills High School. The last SUV pulled away from the curb. The sun was low on the horizon while Lennox and Fulin waited for Hobby Glover to leave the building.

They followed Glover as he drove two miles past the Audubon Society up a forest road where he parked in a turnout. They hung back long enough for him to lock his car and start down the trail. It didn't take long to catch up with him.

When they did, you had to hand it to Hobby, he was quick to realize how pissed off she was. More than your common garden variety pissed off; she wanted to give him some of his own treatment. See how he liked getting the shit knocked out of him, his pants pulled down and someone forcing themselves into him.

But it wasn't Lennox that seemed to really scare the bejesus out of Glover; it was Fulin Chen. Glover let out a howl, a good one. The thing was, they were in a 4,800-acre wilderness down a seldom-used road. All the howling in the world wasn't going to help him much.

Fulin shoved him hard and told him in a deadly voice to shut the fuck up. "Don't make me tell you again."

Hobby tripped and landed in a heap. Fulin yanked him up by his collar and set him back on his feet, stumbling down the Trillium Trail.

The woods grew darker and a light rain began to fall. As they hiked deeper into the park, the only sounds were the drops of rain falling from the forest canopy, and Glover sniveling. It was hard to keep your mad on in all that fresh air and beauty, but Glover's weeping helped her focus. A mile down a wooded hill, they came to an opening. "Here," Lennox said.

Fulin grabbed Hobby by both shoulders and made him face Lennox. There's nothing like a woman full of righteous rage. One look at her mad, beat-up face and he knew his ass was grass.

"You're going to let him kill me," he hiccuped, his eyes going from her face to Chen's. Why was he so crazy scared of Fulin?

"Did you send that man to beat and rape me?" she said.

His face crumpled and a tear rolled down his fat, Humpty Dumpty cheek. Not because she was hurt, but because he was going to be.

"You went to my wife. You were going to blackmail me." He started crying for real now. "I just wanted you to leave me alone."

"Is that what happened to Matilda?" Lennox said. "Did you send some pervert out to hurt her and he killed her instead? Or did you intend to kill her?"

Fulin leaned against the trunk of a large tree, his arms crossed, looking like he could spring to action in less than a heartbeat.

Glover shook from fright, tears running down his face. "No," he blubbered. "I swear I had nothing to do with Matilda's death."

"You knew Matilda Bauer was Tildy, the avatar," she said.

"Yes, just like you said."

"What did she have on you?"

"She dressed in her schoolgirl get-up; I spanked her," he said. "That was all. She was almost thirty. I'm not a pedophile."

He spread his hands to empty, snot running down his nose and into his mouth. "I don't have any more money. Please don't kill me."

His eyes were on Fulin. He was pleading with Fulin. Which is when the penny dropped. Glover thought Fulin murdered Matilda. Which totally nixed her theory and pissed her off even more. He was so perfect for Matilda's murder.

"Did you kill Matilda?" she said.

"No!" His frightened glance went first to Fulin, then slid down to his shoes.

Just to make sure she had it right she said, "I've had enough of this guy. You finish the interview, Chen."

Glover's face was sopping with tears and snot. He sobbed like a baby. "No please, I swear. I'm sorry I got you hurt, I didn't mean it. Don't let him kill me."

"Shit!" she said. Glover was telling the goddamned truth.

"Stop your crying, you baby," she said to Glover. "No one touched you. Let's go," she said to Chen.

"What?" Fulin said.

"He didn't murder Matilda," she said.

"How do you know he's not lying?"

"Because he thinks you did it, you idiot."

Glover stood before them, shaking top to bottom.

"Don't think for a minute you're getting out of this scot free," she said, "I'm calling my friend, Fish, from vice, and having you arrested for assault and attempted rape. You can kiss your good job goodbye."

She nodded to Fulin, and they headed back up the trail. Now Glover had something real to cry about.

CHAPTER 34

Lennox opened the door to Suite 310 at Geitner Graphics. Emily Cross was zipping up her jacket, a large green handbag parked on the top of her desk. Emily grew stiff just from Lennox entering the office. Then she noticed Lennox's face.

"What happened to you?" she whispered.

"I got in a tussle," Lennox said. She motioned to Joan's office. "Is Joan in there?"

Emily's eyes were pleading. "Please don't say anything. I'll get fired if you say anything."

"Don't worry, it will be okay," Lennox said. But she knew there was a good chance it wouldn't be okay. She liked Emily, she really did, and she felt sorry for her, but she'd dime out her own mother if it would prove Fulin's innocence.

Joan Strake stepped out of her office in yoga pants and top, her hair pulled in a loose ponytail, a large gym bag slung over her shoulder.

She looked annoyed when she saw Lennox. "You're trespassing," she said.

"Just two questions," Lennox said.

Joan shouldered past Lennox and out the door. "Call security," she told Emily.

Lennox caught her as the elevator door slid open. She joined Joan and three men who looked like executives.

Two of the men said hi to Joan, the other one nodded, then the elevator turned silent as is the general elevator etiquette.

"She had to have a partner. I'm thinking it might be you," Lennox said. Her words ricocheted off the mirrored walls of the elevator. Lennox noted the men's raised eyebrows. "She wasn't bright enough to be in business on her own." The men looked curious, which wasn't a surprise given Joan's status at Geitner Graphics and talk about partners. Lennox met Joan's eyes in the mirror. Her face had notably paled. She nodded slightly at Lennox.

The elevator doors slid open on the first floor. "Where?" Lennox said.

"There's a tea shop around the corner," Joan said.

As the name implied, The Tao of Tea was Asian-themed, furnished with elegant black tables and ink wash landscapes. Chinese flute music floated through the room. With happy hour in full swing all over the city, they had the place to themselves. Still Joan chose a table in the far corner, and ordered a pot of jasmine tea. The watery light rippled across the bamboo floor.

As the waiter left for the kitchen, Joan said, "Why are you harassing me? The police have solved the case. What do you want?"

"I want to know why you kept Matilda on. Why did you even hire her? She wasn't admin material for you."

"I do a certain amount of outreach," Joan said. "I did my best. She didn't work out the way we'd hoped." She was bluffing. She hadn't moved a muscle, but Lennox felt the flat vibration of a lie.

"Be serious," she said. "She worked for you over a year. Her skills were subpar. She missed thirty-six days of work in a year."

Joan's eyes narrowed. "The police have their killer."

The waiter returned with their tea. They stared at each other in silence until the waiter retreated.

"You met with her behind closed doors. A lot."

Joan smiled, a sub-zero chill in her voice. "You've been talking to Emily."

"Matilda ran a number of internet romances that involved false identities and offshore accounts. She wasn't up to that level of computer sophistication."

"What are you saying?"

"What I said in the elevator," Lennox said. "She had a partner. I think it was you."

For a moment Joan's eyes unfocussed, then she seemed to make up her mind. "We were partners in a way," she said. "We were lovers."

What the hell? If Joan was telling the truth, the only people who knew Matilda and weren't sleeping with her were Emily and Fulin, and she wasn't even sure about Emily. She hadn't thought to ask.

"I thought your tastes ran to younger men," Lennox said.

Joan shrugged. "Mattie was special."

"I don't believe you," Lennox said.

"That we were lovers?"

"That you weren't business partners," Lennox said. "Your ex has left you without the funds to retire. Your salary is not enough."

Joan did a damned good job of looking indifferent.

"You've got nothing to tie me to Matilda other than our work relationship."

"Where were you on Sunday, March 4th?"

"Oh, you want an alibi," Joan said. Her mouth curved in a superior smile. "I was at Cannon Beach, Ocean Lodge from Friday until Tuesday when Emily called me on my cell, told me that Matilda had died. You can check the front desk and they'll confirm. I drove back to Portland Tuesday after Emily's call. Now I've told you everything."

"No, you haven't," said Lennox. "You haven't told me why you kept her on."

Joan reached into the gym bag at her feet and pulled out her cell phone, gave Lennox one long look, then took a candid of Lennox sitting across the narrow table from her. "Geitner Graphics is a secure building. The next time you break into our building, I'll do my best to get you arrested for trespassing," she said.

Maybe Joan and Matilda were lovers. But Joan didn't strike Lennox as a woman who would allow anyone to interfere with her business. And she was a woman who needed to get more serious about her retirement. Could Lennox imagine Joan coaxing Matilda into the naughty-baby outfit and up on a stool? Absolutely.

CHAPTER 35

Lennox left the Tao of Tea and climbed into her Bronco. It was six o'clock, pitch dark, and pouring rain.

If the motive was jealousy, then one of two scenarios had to have played out. One was premeditated. The lover found out he or she wasn't exclusive and set Matilda up. Or the lover found Matilda getting kinky with the one she was cheating with and lost it. If that was the case, where was the one Matilda was cheating with? All of Matilda's lovers had to know what she was like. Lennox hated jealousy as a motive; it was so slippery.

She crossed the Hawthorne Bridge, the struts of the bridge outlined in white lights that flickered in the gloom. Her cell phone rang. It was Jerry.

"I just saw your friend, Tommy, with that cute little reporter, the one making so much trouble for Chen."

"Where?" she said.

"The No-Name Lounge, you know it?"

She didn't. Jerry gave her the address, told her it was downtown, a half a block from Hamburger Mary's on the same side of the street.

Lennox got herself turned around and traveled along I-84 westbound, back to downtown.

There was no sign on the No-Name. Lennox checked the window and made out a few candlelit tables. Collapsing her umbrella, she stepped in. This was a date bar, small and seemingly lit exclusively by candles. Booths lined the wall opposite the bar, with a few tables situated in between. The population consisted of eight or nine couples, most of whom were drinking wine. Jazz played in the background, the conversation low and, from what she could hear, full of sweet talk.

Lennox peered at the people seated at the bar and the couples seated at tables and then she saw them in the back booth, Tommy Pavlik and Chrissy Nash. Seated side by side and leaning toward each other. Tommy grinning that predator grin of his, Chrissy doing the soft and sweet young woman thing. Lennox got a few candids on her cell phone and posted them to Facebook before Tommy and Chrissy knew what hit them.

Tommy tried to stand up, but Chrissy had him penned in.

"Relax," Lennox said. "I've already posted these to Facebook. Lots of cop friends on my Facebook, maybe some of them are yours, too."

Lennox wasn't one to gloat, but damn it felt good to nail this guy. He was such a weasel, and such a bad cop. Not just what he'd done to her, but what he'd fed to Chrissy so that she could destroy Chen's reputation. How could a cop do that to a fellow cop?

Tommy looked like he wanted to tear her apart. "Move," he said to Chrissy. Then his eyes shifted from her to someone behind her and he smiled. She glanced back long enough to see a waiter behind her with a tray full of drinks.

Lennox felt the blow before she realized what had happened. Tommy had thrown something at her. It felt like a rock, and knocked her sideways into the waiter. Hard pain bloomed above her temple. She fell; the waiter's tray fell; the drinks fell. She was covered in broken glass from the drink glasses.

Chrissy yelled, "He hit me! He hit me!"

Tommy charged over to Lennox and ripped her cell phone from her hand. He had to be desperate to pull such a move, but who was going to stop him? He banged through the front door, knocking into people on his way out.

Lennox felt a couple of ice cubes drop inside her neckline as she shifted. She put her hand to her head where she was hit and found blood all over her fingers. The waiter bent over her and called to the bartender, told him she was bleeding.

"Don't move" he said. "You've got broken glass."

He picked shards of it out of her hair and off her clothes.

"What did he hit me with?"

"His drink, I'm pretty sure. Are you okay?"

She wasn't sure. She listened to Chrissy cry in the back booth. By now Tommy had gone into her Facebook app and deleted the picture of him and Chrissy.

The bartender came back with two towels. He guided Lennox to a chair. She realized she was bleeding all over herself and the No-Name Bar.

The bartender carefully dabbed at her cut with a wet cloth, got the waiter to get the disinfectant.

"It's not deep," he said. "Do you want us to call

an ambulance?"

She told him no. He told her he thought she was okay, but anything to the head, you bleed hard. He told her to hold the dry towel against the cut.

"I'm calling the police," he said.

She'd love it if they arrested Tommy, but they wouldn't. They'd see it as a misunderstanding between ex-lovers. She told the bartender, "The guy who hit me *is* a cop."

The bartender said, cop or no cop, Tommy was eighty-sixed from the No-Name forever.

Lennox sat at the table and sipped on a glass of ice water, the towel pressed against her head. The pain had receded to a dull headache. Chrissy walked over to Lennox's table and sat down across from her like she weighed 230 pounds.

"I've never been hit in my whole life," Chrissy said. She pressed a bag of ice against her bruised mouth. Her expression was total outrage. "Tommy lost it when you took our picture."

"Don't you get it? Tommy feeding you privileged dirt is completely unethical. And you ruined Fulin's reputation before he was even tried," Lennox said. "Don't you think that's somewhat worse than me taking a picture of the two of you?"

Chrissy tipped her face like a stubborn child. "Fulin Chen is a pervert."

Lennox looked right into Chrissy's eyes. "You're wrong, and he didn't murder Matilda Bauer. You've hitched your wagon to the wrong star. Tommy is a shitty cop. He always talks about his clearance rate, but check out his conviction stats. They suck."

Chrissy pulled the bag of ice away from her mouth and touched her swollen lip with her fingertips. "I don't even care anymore, I'm done with him. Maybe you're used to violence, but I'm on television."

"So why did he hit you, Miss TV?" Lennox said.

"It was a mistake. He caught me with his elbow. But he didn't apologize, or ask if I was all right. And then he shoved me out of the booth."

"You know he's married."

Chrissy shrugged like a man's marital status was of no consequence. "No one treats me like that," she said.

The only thing that would save this bust hand of a night was getting something out of Chrissy that the woman hadn't already splashed across TV land. Lennox took a deep breath and asked her if she wanted a ride home.

Miss TV sniffed as if Lennox offering to chauffeur her home was the very least Lennox could do. Before they left the No-Name, Lennox left a massive tip for the wait staff, and Chrissy asked for a new bag of ice for her barely swollen lip.

On the walk to Lennox's Bronco, the bulb of inspiration shined down on Chrissy. "I could give this whole thing a spin," she said. "Tell my viewers that while I was investigating a story I was caught in a skirmish."

"Uh-huh," Lennox said.

It started raining again. Lennox had left her umbrella back at the No-Name. She wasn't willing to go back and retrieve it with the Bronco a block from them and the No-Name three blocks behind, Chrissy yammering non-stop about shit that wasn't going to help Fulin's case one single, infinitesimal bit. Thank God Lennox's mother had never gone into show business; she and Chrissy would be the spitting image of "before" and "after."

Lennox and Chrissy were both cold and wet when they

reached Lennox's truck.

"This is your car?" Chrissy said, with enough incredulity she could be Princess Margaret strolling the streets of Portland.

"You don't like the ride, go ahead and order yourself a cab," Lennox said.

Chrissy folded. Big surprise. She made a big deal of climbing into the Bronco, Lennox trying to keep her irritation in check.

So how could Lennox pry Chrissy's mind off herself? Think what worked with Aurora.

Diversion.

Once they were settled in and headed towards John's Landing, Lennox said, "You know, I learned a whole lot from Tommy when I was a rookie. He must've given you this great insight into police investigation."

Lennox glanced at Chrissy in the passenger seat. Chrissy patted her lip with the ice bag.

"Well," she pressed the bag against her lip again. Could she more annoying? "Police work is not like investigative journalism, I can tell you that."

"How so?" Lennox said. *Give me something.*

"Tommy talked about how the simplest explanation usually is the correct one. He said some of his fellow police officers didn't get that. He said they probably watched too many cop shows."

"Did he say I was one of those cops?" Lennox said.

"He never mentioned you," Chrissy said.

CHAPTER 36

When Lennox got home, she checked her Facebook. Sure enough, Tommy had deleted the picture of himself and Chrissy snuggling at the No-Name. The picture had been up on her site maybe five minutes, so the odds that any of her cop friends had caught it before it evaporated into the ether were slim to none. One of these days Tommy would get his skinny ass in a crack that he couldn't wiggle out of. How she was going to love that.

He didn't mention you, Chrissy had said. It shamed Lennox to think she'd been in love with the guy.

The next morning, Lennox's alarm went off at seven. The wind had picked up some time during the night. It dashed rain against her bedroom window. She turned on the lamp and swung her legs out of bed to discover drops of blood on her pillow. She carefully touched the top of her head. Her hair had matted around the wound, but some time during the night, it had stopped bleeding.

Tommy Pavlik. Now they were even: she'd broken his nose a year ago, and he had clobbered her with a drink glass.

Always the one-plus-one guy. *The simplest explanation is the right one.* Chrissy Nash wasn't the only sweet thing who'd heard Tommy's version of investigative method.

It was time to pay another visit to the scene of the crime. Lennox wondered if seven o'clock was too early to call Matilda's mom. Most old ladies get up at the crack of dawn. Lennox decided to give it a shot.

And sure enough, Rose answered on the second ring. Lennox identified herself, told her that they were getting closer to solving her daughter's murder.

"I just want it to be over," Rose said. "I want them to quit talking about Mattie on television."

"It's the same for me," Lennox said. "Not my daughter, I know, but Fulin, he's like my brother. Last night I saw that woman, the one saying all those things on TV, and I think she's going to stop now. Leastways, I think it'll get better."

There was a pause on the line. Lennox looked at the bloodstain on her pillow. A gust of rain smashed against the window.

"Is that why you called?" Rose said.

"I wondered if you'd cleaned out Matilda's bedroom since she passed." Lennox held her breath and prayed to Luck to cut her this one break; she deserved it, goddammit.

A thousand blessings: Rose gave her the answer Lennox wanted. "I haven't been up there. I haven't been able to face it."

Lennox asked her if she could please gain access to the room just this one more time.

Another kiss on the mouth from Mr. Lucky: Rose agreed.

By eight thirty in the morning, Lennox was on the Bauer stoop with a bag of donuts and a grateful smile. The old lady looked like she could use a donut. She'd dropped fifteen pounds at least, poor gal. There was only one way Lennox could help her, and that was to find her daughter's murderer.

Lennox slipped plastic booties and gloves from her bag and put them on before climbing the narrow steps to Matilda's room.

The bedroom wasn't all that different from when Lennox had discovered the body. The hook was still anchored in the ceiling.

Lennox stood beneath the hook and faced the desk. A taller woman standing on a footstool would be in the right sightline for a laptop audience. Lennox slowly turned to the wall behind her to the framed pictures of flowers and kittens from Matilda's childhood. It was the perfect backdrop for Matilda's act.

The room smelled like dirty clothes, the same stale air circulating for the last three weeks. Lennox opened both windows. A gust of rainy wind blew through the room.

Tommy had taken the footstool into evidence along with the contents of Matilda's desk and the file cabinets. Her narrow child's bed had been stripped of bedding. From the discovery documentation, Lennox remembered he'd dusted for prints on the desk, doorknobs, headboard, and stair banister. Matilda's closets were still crammed with clothes, the toy box still filled with Barbie dolls and half-finished coloring books.

Lennox started with the closet, taking out every blouse, every skirt, every dress, looking for a stray hair, anything out of the ordinary. *The simplest explanation is almost always the right one.* It took close to three hours to make it through Matilda's closet. If there was a clue there, it eluded Lennox.

She knelt next to the bed and looked underneath and

came nose to crust with a petrified salami on rye. It looked like Matilda had abandoned it shortly after she'd been paroled. Lennox deposited it on a clean sheet of paper. A year's worth of dust bunnies scattered behind the sandwich like sagebrush.

Then she fished out an empty bag of trail mix and a half-finished bag of corn curls, a six-month-old copy of *People* magazine, and more dust bunnies. A cheap ballpoint pen. Snugged against the foot of the bed was a single gold earring. Lennox changed her gloves before picking it up. It was a small hoop a man or a woman would wear. The hoop was fastened with a y-catch, the kind that sometimes springs, and the earring falls out without someone knowing. How many earrings had Lennox lost over the years? But. But, it could possibly lead to something.

Lennox found Rose in the den, ironing and listening to a couple of women share their experiences with postpartum depression on the tube. Lennox opened her hand and showed the old lady the earring.

"Rose, do you recognize this?" Lennox said.

Rose shook her head.

"Is it possible that it could be Matilda's?"

"It's not Mattie's."

Lennox felt her nerve endings tingle and snap. Hope.

"Mattie didn't have pierced ears," Rose said. "Sure, she got them pierced when she was twelve or so, but they got infected. She was allergic to just about every metal. Eventually the holes healed up."

Lennox wanted to grab the old lady by both shoulders and plant a big, wet kiss on the top of her head. Instead she dropped the earring in an evidence bag and slipped off her gloves. She shook Rose's hand and thanked her for her help and patience.

A small hoop earring. She kept her speed in check, no easy trick when she could finally offer Fulin a shred of bright and shining hope.

It stopped raining momentarily, and Lennox made every green light. She pulled up to the house. Unlocked the front door. Her grin stretched as wide as her muscles allowed.

"Fulin!" she said.

He stood by the fireplace, his cell phone against his ear. "Give me a second," he said into the phone. "I have to write this down."

"Who is it?" Lennox whispered.

Fulin put his hand up to halt her.

"What's your address?" His pen hovered over the notebook page while he listened.

"Okay," he said. He scribbled "Dodge Park" on the notepad. "When?" he said. "I'm leaving now. And thanks. Thanks a lot."

He clicked the phone off. "We've got our murder witness!"

"There was really somebody there?" she said. Her whole body jittered with excitement. Finally, finally the case was breaking open. The payoff for all the beatings she took, the dead ends she followed. They'd been struggling for so long.

"Who is it?" she said.

"A woman," Fulin said. "She was there. She saw the murder."

"Her name?" Lennox said.

"Where is Dodge Park?" he said.

She grabbed Fulin's arm and gave it a shake. "Fulin! What the fuck is her name?"

"She wouldn't say," Fulin said. "But she named the killer. Joey Tufts."

The hope Lennox had felt dropped like a stone at her feet. What Fulin was offering had danger written all over it. "It's a setup," she said.

All the dirty press, this woman comes forward now. Won't give her name, but shops Joey. Lennox knew it was too good to be true.

"You're wrong about this," Fulin said. "She told me how they staged it. And it was like you figured. 'Joey knocked the computer off the desk before he went after Matilda.' How could the witness know that unless she was there?"

"Why send you out to Dodge Park?" she said. "That's way the hell out and gone."

"She's in hiding," Fulin said. "She's afraid if Joey finds her, he'll kill her, too."

Lennox didn't trust this situation, not at all. But the mystery woman had to be involved in Matilda's murder to give those details to Fulin. Or, if she was working for Joey, why did she shop him?

"Did you check her caller ID?"

"Out of area."

"You don't even have a gun since you were indicted," she said.

"Cooper, I'm going. No matter what you say, I'm going."

"Wait," she said. "I'll get my guns. And I do the interviewing when we get there."

Fulin grabbed his jacket, notebook, phone, and keys. Together they ran through the rain to Fulin's BMW.

CHAPTER 37

Fulin typed Dodge Park into his GPS and pulled the BMW from the curb. A classy-sounding robot with a British accent told him to turn left at the corner. The wipers scraped rainwater from the windshield.

Lennox said, "Tell me everything."

"She said Mattie was setting up the pose for a customer, and meanwhile the witness was fiddling with the computer. Joey just came out of nowhere and went nuts."

Joey was yelling and going after Matilda. "The witness blew out of there. Running for her life is the way she put it."

"I've seen how Joey is when he's annoyed. I'd hate to see him with a full mad-on," Lennox said.

"In nine point five miles take Exit 16," the GPS chimed. Fulin hurtled eastbound.

"We need to find out if this witness was Matilda's partner," she said. "The one that helped her set up the identities and bank accounts." Probably another reason the witness hadn't come forward before now.

It hurt Lennox's heart to want something so bad. *Don't*

count on it; don't believe it's real until everything is nailed down.

They sped along the freeway out of the city, veering north to follow the Columbia River. The rain was too heavy to make out the line of the Cascade Mountains.

"God, I hope she's for real," Lennox said.

"She knew old lady Bauer was at church until late afternoon on Sunday. She was crying, saying she was sorry she hadn't come forward before, she was scared of Joey. Wanted police protection if she was going to testify."

These last three weeks had been brutal. Lennox felt like she'd never worked so hard in her life. All their theorizing was finally slotting together.

"Exit 16, turn right," the GPS said.

They turned onto Troutdale Road. Within a couple of miles, farms replaced the outlying east county suburbs. Christmas tree farms flanked the road, the trees still dollhouse-sized, lined up and pruned into perfect little cones. Grapevines trained along wire frames were still skeletal this early in the season. Occasionally there was an original homestead nestled into a copse of trees amongst the country gentleman manor houses. It stopped raining. Jagged ribbons of blue sky tore through the cloud cover.

The witness could be Matilda's lover, partner, or just a friend with a laptop. Matilda tarted herself up, pulled her panties down, stood on a footstool and posed with a man's tie around her neck. Joey comes up the stairs. Had to be the stairs, because Sally Egan saw a man with long black hair enter the Bauer house. Something to verify with the mystery woman. She flees. Grabs her computer, or not, in which case Joey kills Matilda and leaves with said laptop. Takes it out to some junked out place and runs over it until it's the size of confetti. Calls his boss and gets his alibi nailed down hard.

Please let it be real.

"What else are you going to ask her?" Fulin said.

"I'll ask her what she saw before she ran off. I'll ask her did this earring I found belong to her?" She dug in her bag and waved an evidence bag with an earring sliding along the bottom of it.

Fulin asked what it was, and Lennox gave him the story.

"If this is solid, Joey's alibi will cave," Fulin said. "His boss doesn't want to go down for perjury."

"Maybe it's breaking open," she said. And she felt the hope swelling in her. Maybe this was real.

Fulin made a hard turn onto Lusted Road. The farms dwindled, and the land grew more wooded, the road curving through stands of fir and aspen. Clouds thickened once more and the day grew darker.

Lennox glanced at the speedometer. Fulin was going fifteen miles over the posted.

"Slow down," she said.

Chen backed off the accelerator and apologized. "So I'm thinking I'll introduce you. You're the detective I've hired for my defense. I could maybe take notes while you're interviewing?" She thought that was a great idea. The road grew narrower and the woods thicker.

"My first case," Fulin said. In his voice he was declared innocent. They were partners. Fulin Chen and The Case of the Virtual Girlfriend.

As the road curved, it wound closer to the Sandy River. Suddenly the radio turned itself on, a woman screaming the day's news at a decibel that drilled into Lennox's ears.

"What the hell?" she yelled.

"How did that happen?" Fulin shouted.

Fulin poked the touch screen on his dashboard to

silence it. It kept blaring full volume.

"I can't make it stop," he said.

"Let me," she shouted. "You watch the road." She touched the screen where the radio should power on or off. The screen disappeared. The computer overrode her command.

Then the car alarm sounded and the windows started going up and down by themselves. The car was crazy.

"Do something," Fulin shouted over the din. And God, he sounded scared, his hands white-knuckled around the steering wheel.

The computer ignored her commands. Fear and adrenaline pumped through her body. She clenched her jaw to keep from screaming, pulling on her breath to slow it down. And the road grew narrower and narrower. Fulin's speedometer climbed from fifty to sixty.

"Pull over," she screamed.

"The brakes don't work," he yelled over the noise. "I can't stop!"

"The emergency brake!" she said.

"Shit!" he screamed. "Nothing there."

The car sped up to sixty-eight, yellow curve signs smeared past the windows. Cold wind blew through the car. She lost her nerve and screamed. Both of them screamed over the horn and the radio.

"Jump," she said.

"Are you nuts?"

We're going to die, Lennox thought. *What a shame. What a fucking shame.*

Somehow, Fulin made the turn, the BMW fishtailing into the oncoming lane. The car raked along the Armco barrier. Even with the blare of the radio and horn, she heard the hideous sound of metal chewing metal. And still the car gathered speed.

Fulin next to her, that clear, lovely skin and blue-black hair. How he leaned forward to release his trapped hair when he bluffed at cards.

The cliff on the other side of the barrier dropped steeply to the river. Old growth fir trees grew along the cliff banks.

And then the road straightened. The barrier ended. And the BMW was airborne. It seemed forever before they crashed down the bank and into the thick forest. The last thing she saw was the trees.

CHAPTER 38

It was early morning, near as Lennox could tell, the corners of a strange room still in shadow. The shade was up and rain pelted against the window. She was in a narrow bed with rails, a hospital bed. Her arm, outside a stack of thin blankets, was attached to an IV tree.

The crash. She'd somehow survived, unless lying in a hospital bed with the matriarch of all headaches was heaven. It was like her skull was being crushed from the inside out.

Was she paralyzed? Her mind floated above it all. She touched her head with the fingers of her IV arm. There was a bandage on top of her head. She felt the edges of the bandage. It began above her left ear and left off somewhere on top of her head.

She wiggled her fingers. They worked. She pulled back the blanket and checked out her left arm. It was bandaged from below the shoulder to her wrist. Her ring finger was splinted. A busted finger. She could live with a busted finger.

Lennox levered her bed to a more upright position and saw Aurora tipped sideways in the visitor's chair, a blanket covering her chest and legs. The old lady snorted in her sleep.

Lennox pulled the blanket down her body. Her hospital gown was bunched up by her thighs, but neither leg was in a cast. The left leg was bandaged from her thigh to her knee. She wiggled her toes, and they worked too.

What had happened? The car went crazy. The noise, it was deafening, and she and Fulin were screaming. The car was going faster. Then into the trees.

Her mother sighed, her eyelids fluttered, and she came back into consciousness.

"You're awake," Aurora said. "They told me you were stable, but you didn't wake up. How do you feel?" She kneaded the edge of her blanket, and looked like she was going to cry.

Lennox levered the bed so that she was sitting. "Not so great. But in one piece. How's Fulin?"

Tears rolled down Aurora's pale cheeks. She bent down to the foot of her chair, where her black handbag slumped against the chair rungs. She pulled out a tissue and blew her nose. "I'm sorry," she said. "I know he was your friend."

All shreds of detachment evaporated. The room sharpened to brilliant pixels of light. A big surge of "no" was building in her belly and rising. "Spit it out," Lennox told her mother. "What do you mean you're sorry?"

"He didn't make it," Aurora said.

"You mean dead? Fulin?" That was totally impossible. They'd broken the case. They were partners. How could she come out barely scratched and Fulin die? "I don't believe you, Aurora," she said.

Her mother was crying for real now. Total waterworks. What was left of last night's mascara ran down along the fault lines in her face.

Maybe Lennox was dead, too. And this was some kind of weird last bit of consciousness dreaming, she and mother together like in the beginning when she was born. Lennox couldn't bear it.

"I hate you," Lennox said. "Go away."

Aurora leaned closer and squeezed Lennox's hand. "You don't hate me, darling."

Her mother leaned even closer; her sour sleep breath fell on Lennox's face. Aurora was crying harder and Lennox, for once, did not turn away.

"They told me you and Fulin had been life-flighted to Emmanuel Hospital," Aurora said. "I said to them, *is she alive, is she alive?* When I got down here they told me you'd been in a terrible crash and they were running tests on you. They wouldn't let me see you."

Aurora drew a shuddering breath. Lennox's eyes teared up. Fuck, she hadn't cried since she was in third grade. Aurora swiped under her nose with the back of her hand and went in search of the tissue box. That moment when her mother's back was turned was Lennox's chance to take herself in hand. But the harder she tried to keep it in, the harder the pain pushed to get out. A sob broke from the pain in her belly, and Lennox cried for real.

The two of them, Lennox and her mother, crying like it was the end of life and love and everything good.

CHAPTER 39

Detective Richard Sloane rapped twice on Lennox's half-opened door. His small gray eyes swept Lennox and her mother's tear-swollen faces.

"Ohhhhh," he said to Lennox. "You been crying, tough guy?"

"Dick the dick," Lennox said and blew her nose.

Her insult bounced off him without a ghost of a reaction.

Detective Sloane used to be partners with Tommy until after the Pike murder when he put in for a transfer. Even Dick the dick couldn't stomach Tommy, but that didn't make him more likable. His nose and chin competed for room in his long, very long face. He had horse teeth, yellow and flat, and a large shambling body to go with his giant head.

"I'm here to take your statement," he said. He glanced at Aurora. "We need some privacy, ma'am. You mind going out for coffee or something? This'll take twenty minutes tops."

Aurora looked Lennox's way. "Will you be all right?"

"Yeah. He's ugly," Lennox said. "But not dangerous."

"Careful, Cooper, I am still an officer of the law."

Aurora drug her feet like she was being pushed from behind and against her will. When she reached the door, Sloane told her to close it behind her.

"First of all," he said. "You and Chen checked out clean on the blood alcohol tests." Like Lennox should be relieved.

"Of course we did," Lennox said. "The car went crazy."

"Yeah, that happens when you drive over the posted speed," Sloane said.

"It wasn't like that. The computers in the car went apeshit. The radio turned itself on full blast, the car alarm went off, the car accelerated. Fulin didn't even have his foot on the gas pedal. The brakes didn't work."

"Damn computers." His expression read: *I'm dealing with a hysterical woman.* She'd seen his interview techniques plenty of times before; he always gave off the vibe that he didn't believe the person he was interviewing. One of the many attributes that made Dick the dick. He hauled up a deep breath, his gaze drifting to the rain splashed window, and said, "Chen was under a lot of strain. The press, the trial."

"Chen was fine. Chen wasn't the problem," Lennox said. "We had a lead. We were going out to interview a witness."

"Witness?" Now Sloane was interested.

"A woman called Fulin, told him she witnessed Matilda Bauer's murder. She saw Joey Tufts kill the victim."

"Name?"

"She wouldn't say." Lennox felt the skepticism coming off Sloane without having to look at him. She said, "Well, not over the phone, but she gave us Joey Tufts' name."

"So you were deep in East County, tracking down a witness?" he said.

Tracking down a mystery witness. The caller could've been anyone in the world. Lennox and Fulin were betting blind. But she wasn't ready to admit it, not to Dick the dick.

"Yeah," she said. "The case was breaking, I had new evidence, too. You know Tommy, what a sloppy detective he is."

"Yeah, I know Tommy." Sloane sucked his big yellow teeth. "Chen, was he your boyfriend, too?"

"Go fuck yourself."

"Respect, Cooper," he said, his voice as flat as his teeth. "I'm not going to tell you again."

He jotted a note in his notebook and looked up. "What was the last thing you remember from the crash?"

"Like I said, the car went nuts. It kept going faster with no brakes. Are you writing this down, Dick? We made it through the curve, but we were going too fast. We went off the road into the trees."

Dick the dick shook his long horse face at her. "See, right there. You're full of shit, Cooper."

"Respect, Sloane," she said.

"You came in with a concussion. In shock. Now you're telling me you remember everything before the crash."

"Well, I do."

Sloane was shaking his big head.

"Shut up, it happens," she said. "I'm not the only one in the world who remembers something traumatic."

Sloane folded back his notebook and tucked it into the pocket of his tan sports jacket. "Okay, I guess that's it."

He stood up, smoothed his tie. Gold diamonds on a dark polyester background.

"Are you even going to put it in your report, that the car's computers caused it to lose its brakes and accelerate?"

"Yeah, sure thing."

"I want to see Fulin," Lennox said.

That stopped Sloane cold. He stood there looking at her with what might have been a trace element of sympathy. "Trust me, Cooper, you don't," he said. "A tree limb went through the windshield. All I can say is he probably didn't know what hit him. And he won't have to stand trial."

"The trial," she said. She'd forgot.

"That's right," he said. "There is no trial."

• • •

The alarm attached to the IV tree was beeping its head off by the time a nurse entered Lennox's room. Lennox sat on the edge of the bed, her scratched and bandaged legs dangling over the side. She clutched a handful of tissues against her arm.

The nurse saw the limp IV feed, the needle and the tape, all of which should be attached to Lennox, sprawled on the bed.

"What's going on?" she said in a stern voice.

"I'm checking myself out," Lennox said.

The nurse tapped a code on the computer stationed in the corner of the room. She said, "Doctor Weksler wants to keep you another night for observation."

"I need to get back to work," Lennox said.

"You need rest," the nurse said.

"I'm fine. And you know what? This so-called accident is anything but. Someone messed with the computer in Fulin's car to kill him so there'd be no trial. But I'm not quitting, not until it's settled."

The nurse looked like she was witnessing a patient

having a stroke.

"You can't leave without the doctor's orders," the nurse said.

"Watch me," Lennox said.

CHAPTER 40

Lennox shook the broken glass out of her boots into the waste paper basket and pulled them over her nonskid hospital socks. She looked at herself in the mirror. Fat lip, bandaged head, hospital gown, and boots. The way she looked, trying to walk out of here in a backless hospital gown, she'd be lucky to not end up in the psych ward. Aurora's chartreuse coat was draped across the visitor's chair. It was too small, but at least it covered her ass.

Aurora stepped into the room and took in a breath. "Oh my," she said.

"Please don't argue, Aurora, just get the car. I've got to get home."

They rode the elevator down together. Ham, Jerry, Sarge, and Fish met them in the lobby, Ham clutching a giant bouquet of purple and yellow flowers. He took one look at her bandaged head and her bare legs sprouting out of her cowboy boots.

"Where do you think you're going, cowgirl?" he said.

"I told her to stay," Aurora said. "She has a concussion."

Jerry rushed over to Lennox. "You have to get back to your room," he said. "Rest." He looked like he wanted to cry, but being Jerry, he couldn't. And Lennox would be double-damned if she'd start bawling again.

Lennox let herself be comforted for a moment, then took a step back and said, "This was sabotage, guys. Don't think it wasn't. It was the car's computer. Fish, Sarge, you need to check it out. Tell the forensic guys."

"The car techs are on it," Fish said. "We'll have the preliminary results in a week."

"Not good enough," Lennox said. "I'm not going to wait a week for what I already know is true. I was there. We were set up by this chick who said she was a murder witness. So we drive out to East County. When we get to the switchbacks, the car starts acting crazy. Accelerating, windows going up and down, the car not responding. You've never seen this before."

Ham quickly glanced at the other guys, then said in a reasonable voice, "You have a concussion, Lennox. You need to get back to your room. Once the doctors release you, we'll help you. We'll all help. We'll do everything we can."

The guys all nodded their heads, exchanging looks. It wasn't like they didn't want to believe her story that this was a setup. But it was a crazy story. She had a concussion. They'd all lost Fulin.

"Thanks Hammy," she said. "But I'm not waiting for a day or two. Aurora, get the car."

A couple of CNAs and the two women at the reception counter gave her the stink-eye as Lennox limped past the guys out through the glass doors. Nobody stopped her.

Aurora touched her sleeve gently, and Lennox opened her eyes. They were in Lennox's driveway. She climbed up the porch steps with difficulty and fiddled her keys. Inside, the familiar smell of wood smoke and sandalwood. Her leg still hurt like the devil, but her headache eased a few notches.

Aurora wanted to settle her on the sofa. It would feel so good to sink into the cushions.

"You should've gotten painkillers before you left," Aurora said.

"I'll be fine with ibuprofen," Lennox said.

"Can I heat you some soup?"

Lennox told her mother she just needed rest and promised to take an aspirin and lie down. "Thanks, Mom," she said.

"You haven't called me Mom since you were in seventh grade."

Lennox's eyes filled with tears. "I'm sorry," she said. What a shit she was.

"Please darling," Aurora said. "I could've lost you. Please consider doing something else for a living."

They'd had this conversation a hundred times.

Her mother twisted her hand in Lennox's and squeezed. "We'll talk about it later."

Lennox was sorry. It would have been better if she could accommodate her mother and teach school or be a therapist. The old lady spent the night in the hospital, and Lennox said she hated her. And just now Lennox lied. She had no fucking intention of taking a little nap. She was going to find out who killed Fulin or go down trying.

Lennox shrugged out of Aurora's coat and helped her mother into it. Watched Aurora drive away. Then walked into her office and typed "car computers" into her search engine. What came up were performance chips—something you could swap out of your car to modify the engine's power. The fools that screech out when the stoplight turns green? Odds were the winner had chipped his engine. Any one could buy a chip and have it installed for just under a grand. Could a chip override the driver's commands?

Al Paulson owned a sports car garage. Lennox had no idea if Debbie even knew Fulin, much less had his unpublished number, but it was a hell of a coincidence, Al being in the business. Plus she'd found out that he was having issues with the state regarding compliance.

Lennox pulled her leather jacket on over her sweats and locked up the house. The meds they'd given her in the hospital were wearing off. She could barely walk to her Bronco much less get in it. She gritted her teeth and drove to Paulson's Imports.

The place was a one-story, flat-roofed garage with three garage doors. The paved yard was surrounded by an eight-foot cyclone fence topped with a roll of razor wire. The minute she parked the Bronco, she could hear rap music thumping from the open stall. The gate was unlocked. Lennox counted eleven cars in the yard, all Mercedes and older Alfas. As she got closer to the garage, she could smell machine oil and tires.

The mechanic was working on a baby blue Mercedes sedan that looked older than Lennox. On the wall behind him was a poster of a topless model pretending to wax an Alfa. The mechanic wiped his hands on a rag.

"Do you install performance chips?" she said.

The kid turned his attention to her Bronco. "Not in that antique," he said.

"What about a BMW?"

"Sure," he said. "All the time."

"What about custom work," she said. "Can you change

229

the way a car responds?"

The kid shrugged. "What do you want your car to do?"

"Accelerate without using the gas pedal?" she said. "Make the brakes not respond?"

The kid looked scared. He knew what she was talking about, but he shook his head, his lips pressed together. He pointed to the office.

Al Paulson stood behind the counter of a tweed-carpeted office. Opposite the counter, two visitor chairs faced a wall-mounted television set. He looked up from his laptop with a big old smile ready on his face.

Watch his smile vanish when he recognized her.

"I only have a couple questions. It won't take five minutes of your time," she said. "I understand you install performance chips."

Al shut the lid of his laptop with a click. "Are you looking to buy a performance chip or you just snooping?"

"Your butt's in a sling," she said. "You've employed Lyon and Welsh to defend you in a compliance issue."

He pointed to her beat-up face. "Looks like someone stuck her nose in the wrong guy's business."

"Are you threatening me?" she said

"All I'd have to do is blow and you'd fall over," he said.

"I'm packing," she said.

"Look, there's nothing against the law in swapping out performance chips. Lots of garages do it," he said.

Sure, he was angry; he was in trouble; he'd got caught with his hand in the cookie jar. Lennox could see him fudging the books. What about murder? Debbie was his meal ticket. If someone jeopardized her business, what would he do to protect hearth and home?

"You say lots of garages do it. Name some," she said.

Gallagher's Performance, Basko's Imports, Superior Auto, Bendix Motors.

She wrote the names in her notebook. Head to foot, her body was one long ache. She had to get the hell out of there before she passed out.

She hobbled back to her car and drove home. Limped into her house, and made straight to the cupboard with the Jack Daniels. Not a painkiller invented that did the job of a shot of Jack. Maybe two shots.

* * *

Lennox woke up the next morning feeling like she'd been run over by a very large truck. She had face-planted on top of her bed, still fully clothed, still with her boots on. Clinging to the banister, she reached the bathroom. She was too weak to stand up in the shower. Okay then; she'd take a bath. And ibuprofen. Coffee. She'd visit the other garages Al Paulson listed. By the end of the day she'd know how someone could've messed with the BMW's computer.

Lennox wiped the steam from the bathroom mirror and looked at her face. She had a black eye and the top and side of her head was bandaged. She slowly unwrapped her head. They had shaved most of her hair, front and side. The stitches ran from behind her ear to the other side of her head.

She turned the water off and got herself some scissors. Cut the rest of her hair off. Then shaved her scalp smooth. She looked like she'd been to war and lost. But she had one more battle in her, and nobody was going to stop her.

She drove to Gallagher's on southeast Pine and 20th. They didn't have anything for her. Struggling back into the

Bronco, she swallowed more pills, then headed further south to Basko's Imports. The young guy fixing a '78 Porsche was also the owner. He wore gray coveralls, had thick sandy hair and a cute smile. He told her he could install a performance chip, but really, if she wanted more power she'd be better off buying a car with a bigger engine. She decided to take a chance on this guy, and she described the crash to him.

"You're not talking about chipping an engine," he said. "What you're talking about is hacking a car. There was this guy I heard about up in Seattle drove right off the pier into the Puget Sound. They said his car was hacked."

He rubbed his hands on the front of his coveralls and shook his head. "What you're looking for is a computer geek, not a wrench head."

CHAPTER 41

One in the morning, Lennox trying her hardest to get some sleep. Her heart started to hammer against her ribcage. She grew short of breath. Was she having a heart attack? She pulled herself to a sitting position, reached for the ibuprofen bottle and finished the water on her night table.

Her chest tightened as if her ribs had collapsed and were pressing against her heart and lungs. If only she would've listened to her nurse, stayed in the hospital for observation. Her dad died of a heart attack. She was all alone. Of course that was the way she'd go. Alone.

She felt her pulse hammer inside her wrist. This was so wrong. Symptoms of heart attacks in women? She had no idea. She got out of bed. She felt light-headed. She tried to breathe. Take small breaths. Sips. Lennox clutched the banister with one hand, the wall with the other. Tried not to pass out and fall down the stairs. Mother of Christ, what was happening to her?

She made it down the stairs, down the hall to her computer. Typed "symptoms female heart attack." Then the pain, the shortness of breath, all that pressure lifted as suddenly as it had come on. She sat in her office chair staring at her computer screen, waiting for the pain to begin again. But it didn't. She was back to her leg aching, the dull headache along her scalp.

Maybe a cup of tea. Check the door locks. Lennox walked past Fulin's room. The smell of the sandalwood incense he always burned. The smell that seeped into his clothes and his hair. How could he be gone? She walked into his room. The unmade bed. His biker boots on their sides by the chair. Centered on the dresser was the elephant-headed god, Ganesh, remover of obstacles, god of luck. She didn't know the story of why a Chinese guy favored a Hindu god, but Luck was a guy they all prayed to. You can't play cards and not believe in him.

She held Ganesh's brass body in her hand and closed her fingers around him. He was ridiculous, with his elephant head and potbelly. Dancing on his human legs, the dance that goes on endlessly, no matter how many drop away. Fulin said he was potent. She rubbed her finger over his potbelly, and asked the little guy for luck. Lit a stick of incense, set it in Fulin's onyx holder.

"Find the person who killed him," she said to Ganesh. Ganesh seemed to look at her with his small elephant eyes. She watched the smoke spiral towards the ceiling.

Your prayers to the gods are carried on the smoke, Fulin had said.

Fulin's turquoise leather jacket hung on the hook behind the door. Lennox slipped in her arms, zipped the jacket to her chin. She hadn't realized how cold she was until she put it on.

Then she was tired. So tired she would never make it

upstairs. She eased herself into Fulin's bed. The sheets and the blankets smelled of him. Floating in a world of Fulin. She started to sob, and once she started she couldn't stop.

CHAPTER 42

Fulin. He was the first thing in her head when she woke the next morning, her eyes gluey from all the tears. Enough with the tears; what she wanted was justice. She'd clear his name whether anyone believed her or not, whether she got help or not. It took ten minutes to stand up from Fulin's bed and onto her stitched-up leg. More pills, then the coffee pot, her standard breakfast these days. She watched the hail ping off the windowsill. A lonely daffodil by her driveway lay flattened under a thin blanket of ice.

She took her coffee and went to the office. Twelve messages blinked on her machine. She ignored them and called the Seattle Police asking for the cop in charge of cyber crime.

"Paul Linder," the cop said.

She identified herself, told Linder that she and Fulin Chen were investigating a murder, and then she described how the car behaved before they crashed.

"Investigating officer?" he said.

"Richard Sloane."

Officer Linder told her he'd make some calls and get back to her. An hour later he called and told her he was on the road headed for Portland. When could he see her?

"As soon as you get here."

She gave him her address and went out on the porch to fetch the newspaper. A two-foot teddy bear sat propped by her door, splashed with Cory Doran's fake blood. Blood splatter on a greeting card addressed to her. She'd lost Fulin, and this little jerk continued to harass her.

So sorry about Fulin, the card said. *Hope you're okay.* Frank. What a good man. Fulin had always made him feel uncomfortable. She did too, when it came to that. He didn't want to see her anymore, but still he could be nice about it. Write that he was sorry. Send her a teddy bear of all things. He never did get her.

Dealing with Cory would have to wait. Lennox retreated to the kitchen for the scrub bucket and paper towels. Her headache had eased, but her leg still stung with every movement. She was showered and dressed by the time the doorbell rang. Ham stood at her front door. He held a handle bag, looking as beat and desolate as she felt.

"Meghan made you some soup," he said. Lennox didn't know that Meghan could even cook. She let him in. He managed to hug her, checking in with every body part before touching her. Back? Okay. Arm? Better not. Somehow he encircled her, the handle bag swinging from his fingers.

"I'm expecting a cop any minute," she said. "He investigates cyber crime up in Seattle."

"I won't keep you then," Ham said. "But I've got something other than soup for you. Before Hobby Glover worked at Cedar Hills High, he was vice principal at Rosemont High. Emily Cross was a student there."

"Emily could've known that he was kinky," Lennox said. "Could've set him up to be blackmailed."

Ham set the soup on the dining room table.

"Call me when you're done with the cop," he said.

• • •

Paul Linder stood on her freshly washed welcome mat, five foot five, and weighing under 150. He had very blond hair, and blond eyelashes with the lightest blue eyes she'd ever run across. And young. Lennox's paperboy could be this guy's big brother. He showed her his badge and she asked him in.

He accepted her offer of coffee, and pulled a computer from his briefcase. No notebooks for this guy; he was a cyber-crime dude. He verified that Fulin was driving the car at the time of the crash and then he asked her to repeat the events leading up to the car leaving the road. This was all stuff she had told him on the phone, but she recounted again how it all started with the radio. The sound was deafening, she told him.

"You didn't have the radio turned on before it went full blast?" He had a deep voice for such a young guy.

She told him no, and neither she nor Fulin could turn it off. Then the car alarm sounded off.

"The radio was still going?"

"Yeah, then the windows. Up and down, up and down. It was totally crazy, and there was nothing we could do to stop it."

"Mr. Chen was driving," he said. "He was trying to turn off the radio etc. Was he panicked? Did he still have control over the car?"

"At that point, we were both scared. I don't think either of us had panicked yet," she said. "Fulin said he was going to pull over. I watched him stand on the brake, but the car just went faster."

They were going over sixty when they hit the curves. The last thing she remembered was the guardrail and going over the bank.

Linder looked up from tapping on his tablet. "Forensics retrieved the car's black box. Classic hack," he said. "If I'm right about this, it's the third case I've run across in the Northwest. The business with the radio, the alarm, all that's new. You're the first eyewitness that's survived." He looked at her like she was a precious jewel. It wasn't a look she was used to unless she was in bed. He said, "Tell me why the two of you were driving out in the country."

"Fulin got a phone call from a woman," she said. "She wouldn't give her name, but claimed to have witnessed the murder."

"The Bauer murder," Linder said. His expression remained neutral, but obviously he must've gotten the whole story from Dick the dick. She waited for the follow up questions: was Chen depressed, had he expressed any suicidal thoughts, but Linder didn't go there. He just typed away on his tablet.

"The woman on the phone named Joey Tufts as the murderer."

"Your suspect?" he said.

"One of them. She said she was staying at her cousin's cabin on the Sandy River, which is why we were out there."

He produced an Oregon map from his briefcase. He had marked Fulin's route from the freeway to the crash site, his finger tracing the line from the freeway down

Lusted Road to where it changed from straight to hairpin switchbacks through the forest.

"That's right," she said.

"There's basically one efficient way to get from your place to Dodge Park which is how this hack works. The hacker calculates the GPS distance to where the road gets dangerous. Then when you reach it, the program overrides the car's computer, causing it to accelerate, etc., etc."

"So how did he hack into Fulin's car?" she said.

"Somebody has to be able to get physically inside the car. He attaches his external drive to the CAN-bus port under the dashboard and uploads the program. The whole thing takes seven minutes, tops."

She must've looked confused about the CAN-bus thingie, so he explained it was the port that connected everything electronic in the car. "It's what they plug into when you get a smog test," he said.

"Does the hacker have to do it himself, or could anyone attach the drive to the CAN-bus?"

"Anyone who could slim-jim a car," he said.

"What about the emergency brake?" she said.

"No, that wasn't the hack," Linder said. "Probably the person who slimmed the car cut the brake cable."

Joey Tufts could slim a car. Could Debbie? Probably not, but her husband could. What about Joan? Emily?

She asked him what kind of skill would it take to hack a GPS.

"This is not just somebody good with computers, or even a programmer working as an assassin on the side. We're talking a highly skilled specialist, which is why I think it's the same guy responsible for the vehicular deaths in Seattle, Boise, and now Portland. They've all happened in the last six months."

Linder drained the last of his coffee. "We haven't talked about motive," he said.

"One of the suspects in the Bauer murder wanted to kill Fulin," Lennox said. "Which would stop the investigation. She hires the hacker, takes out Fulin, end of story."

"She being the woman who sent you out to Dodge Park?"

"Has to be. Doesn't it?"

"I don't know," he said. "You're the homicide detective."

Who else but Matilda's murderer would've set Fulin up? Or was her theory wrong-headed?

"One thing I can tell you is that this kind of murder doesn't come cheap," he said. "Look for someone who wanted the kill to look like an accident and had the money to hire our guy."

Joey could've slimmed the car, but only Joan or Debbie could pull up the funds.

"Is there anything more you can tell me," he said. "Any impressions we might not have talked about?"

She told him no. He reached in his pocket and wrote down his cell number before handing her his business card.

"You might think of something more. Call me any time," he said.

He reached out to shake hands. She was so grateful to be believed, to actually share inside information with a cop, she kept shaking his hand, and shaking it.

"You were lucky," he said.

She dropped his hand. The heaviness she'd woken up with returned. "The last thing I feel is lucky."

CHAPTER 43

She was alive. Was that all she could say for her luck? Fuck it then. Back to police procedure all the way. She had the training, the brains; she didn't have to rely on luck. Fulin would not go down in people's memories as a rapist and a murderer.

It was six in the morning, the sky just starting to lighten in the east. Lennox hauled herself into a rented Honda Civic, an automatic tranny so she didn't have to clutch with her bad leg. The leg ached clear down to the bone. She headed to Joey Tufts' house in the Flats.

The mystery woman who'd lured Fulin to Dodge Park had named Joey as Matilda's killer. Joey may have not killed Matilda, but he was involved up to his neck. Fulin kept his BMW out on the street in front of Lennox's house. Joey knew where she lived. It made sense that Joey had slimmed Fulin's car, cut the emergency brake cable and attached the hacking laptop to Fulin's CAN-bus.

Which of the suspects partnered with Joey? Whoever the mystery woman was, she hadn't counted on Lennox continuing the investigation. The suspect had to be worried sick on account of Joey being too stupid to hold up under scrutiny. And Lennox would tail him forever until he led her to his partner.

It was still quiet and sleepy when Lennox pulled into Joey's neighborhood. Only one house besides Joey's had its lights on. Lennox unholstered Old Ugly, her service revolver, and aimed it at his front door. She'd love to shoot the bastard. Kneecap him so he'd be in continual pain for the rest of his sorry life. She laid the gun on the seat and dug through her bag for more ibuprofen. Just as she swallowed the pills, Joey left his house. He loped down his sidewalk swinging his arms, more relaxed than she'd ever seen him. What did he have to be relaxed about? The pills stuck in her throat.

Lennox followed him west along Powell, left on Cesar Chavez. It was fully light, raindrops glistening off the bare branches in the sunlight. Joey jogged right on Cora Street and parked in front of a siding tear down. She parked down the street, but still close enough to get a good view of the construction site. She watched Joey and the other men as they pried off rotting stucco. Do that eight hours a day and a mind could start thinking about easier ways to make a buck. Especially a mind like Joey's.

Eight long hours. Lennox took a couple of bathroom breaks, her body hardly able to stand straight, much less walk. Back at the construction site, she ate sandwiches and drank bottled water. Rubbed her knees and lower back. At five o'clock, Joey jumped in his truck and maneuvered down Powell Boulevard. The traffic thinned as they headed into East County. Twenty minutes later, he pulled into The Copper Penny. Lennox called Fish and told him to drive to the bar on the double. "I'm in a silver Honda parked across the street," she said.

Ten minutes later Fish parked his Jeep behind her car. He patted her head through the open window. "Does it hurt?" he asked.

Of course it hurt.

Lennox gave Fish Joey's description. Told him to sit as close to Joey as possible. If Joey was there with anyone, Fish was to eavesdrop if he could. Lennox said, "The beer's on me." Fish told her he didn't need her damned money. His face flushed darker. "I told you I'd help. I meant it," he said.

Forty-five minutes later, Joey left the bar. Lennox started her car and followed him down Powell. Her phone rang.

"Was he with anyone?" she asked Fish.

"No. Now what?"

"He's probably going to head home," she said. "I'll watch the house until he goes to sleep."

"Let me do that," he said. "You know, Cooper, I didn't want to say it, but you look like shit."

She could argue with him, but truth was, she was hard-pressed to find one square inch of her body that didn't hurt. She gave Fish Joey's address, in case Fish lost him.

"Like I can't run a tail," he said. "Fuck you."

They agreed to talk first thing in the morning unless something came down, in which case he would call in the troops. She could always count on good old Fish.

The night passed uneventfully.

At six the next morning, Lennox hauled her aching ass into her rental car. Once again she followed Joey to work, and followed him to The Copper Penny after. This time Fish was parked in the lot before she got there. He took over the night shift, promising to call Lennox if anything happened.

Three days of the same: work, bar, home. They had reached Friday. It was still dark at 6:00 a.m. and raining hard when Lennox got into her car. She drove down Powell listening to the morning news when Fish called her.

"How did it go?" she said.

"Quiet," he said. He had the grace not to whine about all the time wasted watching Tufts.

"I'll take the night shift tonight," Lennox said. "You go play poker."

"Poker's been suspended," Fish said. "No one's got the heart."

"I got a feeling about tonight," she said.

"If something's going down," Fish said. "I want to be there."

"Park back," she said. "He's not as stupid as he looks."

Fish muttered expletives under his breath.

Another day of work. The construction guys troweled cement onto the newly wrapped walls. Eight hours, a peanut butter and jelly sandwich for breakfast, a tuna fish sandwich for lunch. Same old, same old. She rolled down her window, letting the cold air keep her awake. By late afternoon she'd pounded down enough ibuprofen she was afraid for her kidneys.

The crew broke up at five. Slanting light lit the bare trees and houses. She tailed Joey back to The Copper Penny, parked two rows behind Joey's truck in the parking lot, and prepared for another wait.

He was back in his truck twenty minutes later. Tonight was the night. She felt it. She knew it. She drove east, three cars behind Joey, back to Felony Flats.

It was fully dark when Lennox parked two cars from Joey's house. His porch light was out. Lennox watched his living room lights come on. Twelve and a half hours of surveillance behind her, and no idea how many hours ahead. Old Ugly on the seat beside her, her Glock next to Ugly, ready to go.

Nothing happened.

Lennox rubbed her bald head, the stitches rough against her hand.

All the resource, all the effort she spent, and here she was sitting in a rental car, running surveillance on an ex-con in Felony Flats with no result. She hated her job. She hated her luck.

An S-series Mercedes parked in front of Joey's house. Lennox didn't recognize the car. A tall figure in a black leather jacket and a black knit cap climbed Joey's steps and rang the doorbell. Black leather jacket like the guy Sally Egan saw entering the Bauer house on the day of Matilda's murder. Or a woman? Lennox wasn't sure in the dim light.

Where the hell was Fish? Lennox looked in her rear view mirror. No sign of him.

Joey and Black Leather walked together to the back of the Mercedes. Black Leather opened the trunk. Lennox had seen this maneuver before. Did Joey have any clue that he was a liability?

"It's way in the back," a woman said.

Debbie Paulson.

"Can you get it?" she said. Half of Joey's body leaned inside the trunk. She reached into her pocket.

Lennox half leapt, half fell out of the rental car, yelling for all she was worth. "Joey, watch out."

Debbie turned and fired. Flame and the smell of gunpowder. A bullet hit Lennox's windshield.

Lennox knelt behind her open door and yelled,

"Drop your gun."

"Joey, she's trying to kill us," Debbie screamed.

Debbie and Joey ducked behind the Mercedes. With the trunk door open, Lennox lost anything resembling a sight line. She heard Joey say, "Gimme that." Noise like they were struggling. Lennox peeked around her car door. Heard a shot. No more struggle.

Nobody in the neighborhood reacted. No dog even fucking barked. Felony Flats.

Lennox took aim and shot Debbie's trunk door. "Drop the gun, Debbie," she yelled. "The cops are on their way."

A burst of flame. A bullet hit Lennox's door.

Two shots rang from behind Lennox. *Please, oh please, make it the cavalry.* Her ears were ringing from adrenaline and gunfire. Fish dove next to Lennox.

"I called in for backup," he said, heaving for breath.

"It's Debbie Paulson. Reason with her," Lennox said.

"Police," Fish yelled. "Drop your weapon."

A flash of fire, the bullet piercing Lennox's grill.

Then the blessed sound of police sirens coming closer.

What seemed like forever happened in seconds. Debbie's gun skidded across the pavement. She came out from behind the car, hands up, tears running down her face.

"Don't shoot," she said.

There she was crying again. Even in the dark, you could see mascara running down her face. Killed three people and still with the tears. Where she was headed she could have a nice long cry.

Fish was the one that cuffed Debbie and read her her rights.

Cop cars pulled into the street, hemming everyone in. Lennox dropped her gun and put her hands up. Told the cop her PI license was in the car.

"PI." His face looked like he smelled something bad.

"She's okay," said Fish. "She's with me."

Lennox pointed to the Mercedes and told the cop to look for Joey. A few minutes later, an ambulance parked at the scene. Minutes later, two EMTs wheeled Joey's body into the back of their vehicle. A sheet covered his face. Dead. Lennox felt nothing for him. The ambulance left the scene without siren or blinking lights.

She shivered in the whirling blue and red light, waiting to give her statement. Wanting nothing more than a heating pad and a big slug of Jack Daniels. She could almost feel its warmth sliding down her throat. A toast, she'd say. To you, Fulin.

CHAPTER 44

It was drizzling again when Lennox left the Shanty. She opened her umbrella to keep the water off Fulin's turquoise motorcycle jacket. His jacket was way too big for her; the hem floated over her thighs and the sleeves were rolled back twice.

Tonight had been the first poker game since Fulin died. It took her and her pals three months before anyone had the heart to play without him. And by then she was mostly healed.

The Debbie Paulson trial was set for the second week in July. Once Debbie was arrested, she confessed to everything. How she'd been willing to leave her family, her friends, her house, everything to run away with Matilda and start a new life. A new identity where Matilda didn't have a felony conviction or a parole officer. Debbie had her bags packed. She'd emptied her bank accounts, and most of her and Al's investments. When Al left Friday afternoon for Spokane, Matilda came over to the Paulson house. She and Debbie had planned to leave the next day, destination

Atlanta, Georgia. But Matilda came with no luggage, no money. She had cold feet. "If you don't like Atlanta, name the spot. We can go anywhere," Debbie had said. Matilda agreed to return home and pack her things. Sunday Matilda quit answering her cell phone. Debbie went to her house. Wearing a leather jacket, her hair in a ponytail, the witness, Sally Egan, mistook Debbie for Fulin.

Debbie found Matilda upstairs staging a sex act with a live person on the internet. Matilda, the woman Debbie was willing to give up everything for. Debbie kicked the stool over and watched Matilda clawing at the tie around her neck.

She had no alibi, and found it increasingly hard to lie to her husband when he confronted her about Lennox's questions. Debbie had to stop the investigation. She knew a hacker, one of Matilda's friends. A guy who could mess with your car's computers. It cost Debbie $40,000.

Then she had to convince Joey to help her with the car hack.

Matilda, Fulin, Joey—how many more people would she have killed to save herself?

Drizzle turned to rain. Lennox maintained a brisk walk to the corner of Sandy when Fish's twenty-year-old jeep pulled to the curb.

"Let me give you a ride," he said.

She waved him off. "Thanks, I'm okay to walk."

"Yeah, yeah, I know that," Fish said. "But I got something to tell you. Something private."

Old Fish had a secret. Which would explain why he'd twitched all night like he had spiders up his butt, and made so many stupid calls at the card table. He must've lost almost a hundred bucks, and didn't even look bummed.

Lennox could resist nearly everything but a secret.

She collapsed her umbrella and climbed into the truck. It smelled like pepperoni sticks and pine tree deodorizer.

He put the Jeep in gear and said, "You can't tell anybody; it's not official until next week."

"Okay," she said.

"I'm getting promoted to detective."

Lennox squeezed his arm because it was so terrific, so deserved. "You'll make a great detective," she said.

"I told you early," Fish said. "Because you get some of the credit. The Paulson arrest. And the hit-and-run in the Pike case. You're okay, Cooper."

"You too, Fish."

"Something else," Fish said. He glanced over at Lennox. "Tommy's been busted down to patrol cop."

Maybe it was a sign of better times. When rewards went to the deserving and justice was meted out to the guilty. Wasn't that the whole point of being a cop? You have to keep the faith. You have to believe in finding the truth. And do your utmost to see that the wrongdoer is punished. It's what keeps society from falling to pieces. You have to do it because Mr. Luck doesn't give two shits either way. It's a random universe out there. And nothing was going to bring Fulin back.

Fish dropped Lennox off at her house. They said goodnight, and he almost hugged her, but then thought better of it. Lennox unlocked her front door and dumped her bag on the table. She poured herself a glass of pinot and sat in the big chair by the fireplace. She heard the sound of footsteps running up her driveway, and looked out the window.

Cory Doran stood on her porch with a five-gallon bucket. He stood five foot ten. Skinny. John's long thin nose and red hair.

She opened her front door.

"Cory Doran," she said.

All these months he'd been hating someone he'd never laid eyes on. For a moment he forgot to be angry.

She whipped her cell phone from the pocket of Fulin's jacket. "Smile," she said. And took his photo.

"What are you doing?" he said. His face twisted with hate and fear.

You're not doing the kid any favors, Fulin had said.

She squared her shoulders and took a deep breath. It was time.

"Your dad saved my life," she said. "He's a hero. Now, let's go pay a visit to your mom and tell her what you've been up to the last six months."

ACKNOWLEDGMENTS

To Liz, my agent, editor and friend—how lucky I am to have you. To the folks at Diversion Books: Randall, Sarah and Mary—my deep gratitude for your careful attention to *Betting Blind* and for sticking by me when I was sick and slipped my deadline. To Jim Frey, my teacher and dear friend. To Susan Whitcher for the brainstorming, the critique, the gallons of chicken soup and all the other ways you've helped me get through these last two years. My love and gratitude to the Fat Friday writers: Martha Ragland, Barbara Davis Kroon, Susan Whitcher and Caroline Kurtz. To Martha Miller, Susan Clayton Goldner, Dorothy Blackcrow and all the great writers and critiquers that make up FWOF. To Jilly, Mihkel, Bruce, Barbara, Meghan, Kelly, Debbie, Lisa and Mark—your love and support has been invaluable.

And to Michael, my darling man, for all you do.

CPSIA information can be obtained
at www.ICGtesting.com
Printed in the USA
FFOW04n1232110116
20270FF